"I'm pregnant

It was the last thing [   ]
and so it took him a [   ]
revelation.

"You have got to be kidding."

"Do I look like someone performing a comic routine, Sergio? I'm pregnant. I only found out yesterday. I did the test. In fact, I did two tests and there's no mistake. I'm having a baby. I'm having *your* baby."

He vaulted upright, stared at Susie and raked his fingers through his hair. "You can't be." He stood in front of her, feet apart, challenging her to defy that simple statement.

In his heart, he recognized the ring of sincerity and fought against it.

Pregnant? How had that happened? He was going to be a *father*? Even when he had loosely contemplated the idea of eventually settling down with a suitable woman, his thoughts had not stretched into the realms of fatherhood.

His eyes flew to her stomach and just as quickly looked away.

"Don't tell me that *I can't be,*" Susie snapped. She glared at him. Did he think she was lying? No, of course not! He was desperately clinging to denial because the alternative was so hideous that he couldn't bring himself to give it credence. He was a man who liked to control every aspect of his life and just like that, he'd lost it.

Cathy Williams

Bound by the Billionaire's Baby

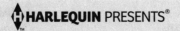

HARLEQUIN PRESENTS®

ISBN-13: 978-0-373-13357-4

Bound by the Billionaire's Baby

First North American publication 2015

Copyright © 2015 by Cathy Williams

Recycling programs
for this product may
not exist in your area.

This edition published by arrangement with Harlequin Books S.A.

For questions and comments about the quality of this book,
please contact us at CustomerService@Harlequin.com.

® and TM are trademarks of Harlequin Enterprises Limited or its
corporate affiliates. Trademarks indicated with ® are registered in the
United States Patent and Trademark Office, the Canadian Intellectual
Property Office and in other countries.

HARLEQUIN®

www.Harlequin.com

Printed in U.S.A.

Cathy Williams can remember reading Harlequin® books as a teenager, and now that she is writing them, she remains an avid fan. For her, there is nothing like creating romantic stories and engaging plots, and each and every book is a new adventure. Cathy lives in London and her three daughters, Charlotte, Olivia and Emma, have always been, and continue to be, the greatest inspiration in her life.

Books by Cathy Williams

Harlequin Presents

Visit the Author Profile page at Harlequin.com for more titles.

To my three wonderful and inspiring daughters

CHAPTER ONE

FROM THE VERY second Susie walked into the restaurant she knew she had made a big mistake. It joined the other three big mistakes she had made in the past fortnight. Making mistakes was beginning to feel like a full-time occupation.

What had possessed her to wear high heels? Why was she clutching a silly little bag with sequins, borrowed from one of her friends? And how on earth had she found herself in a ridiculous small red dress which had screamed sexy and glamorous when she had tried it on earlier in the week but now shrieked…sad and desperate?

Utterly grateful that she had wisely shunned the flamboyant checked coat which she had been tempted to buy with the dress, and had instead chosen something slightly more sober, she wrapped her black cape tightly round her, making sure to conceal every single square inch of the stupid red dress.

So what the heck should she do now? she wondered.

Date number four was there and seated at the bar. In a couple of seconds he would look round and he would spot her. She had told him that she would be wearing red. The red might be concealed under the cape but how many other lonesome single girls were there here? None.

His picture on the online dating agency she used had

seemed so promising, but one glance at him showed her
that it had been a cruel lie.

He wasn't tall. Even though he was sitting she could see
that. His feet *dangled.* Nor was he surfer blond...more wet
sand than surf, to be perfectly honest...and he looked at
least twenty years older than in his photograph. Furthermore he was wearing a bright yellow jumper and trousers
that were vaguely mustard in colour.

She should have actually chatted with him on the phone
instead of rushing headlong into a date. She should have
relied on more than a couple of flirty messages and one
email. She would have known then that he might be
the sort of guy who wore yellow jumpers and mustard-
coloured trousers. But instead she had jumped right in at
the deep end and now here she was...

She felt faint.

This was an expensive bar/restaurant. It was the latest in
hip and cool. People had to wait for months to get a book-
ing. The only reason she had been able to get one was because her parents had had to cancel at the last minute and
had told her that she could go along in their place. They had
asked her to report back on the food—they wanted details.

'Take a friend,' her mother had said, with just the
amount of weary resignation that seemed to hallmark everything she said to her. 'You surely must know *someone*
who isn't absolutely broke...'

By which she had meant, *You must know a man who
isn't scraping by without a decent job...someone who
doesn't play in a band in bars...or doesn't slouch around
in between acting jobs that never come up...or isn't currently saving to go on a world trip, taking in the Dalai
Lama on the way...*

The mere fact that online date number four had heard
of this place had been a point in his favour.

Silly assumption on her part.

Her fundamental sense of decency warred with a pressing urge to turn tail and scarper before she was spotted—but how could she scarper when she knew her parents would want to know all about the experience? It wasn't as though she could wing it…make it up as she went along. She was rubbish at lying and her mother was gifted at spotting lies.

Yet she knew what the outcome of this would be before it even started. She knew they would make stilted conversation but would both be keen to end it. She knew that the conversation would run out sometime after the starter but they would both feel obliged to stay until the main course and she knew they would definitely leave without dessert or coffee. She felt he might make her pick up the tab. He would definitely insist on going Dutch. He would probably work out exactly who had eaten what and calculate the bill accordingly.

Already in the grip of uncertainty and a mild depression that she had found herself in this situation *yet again*, Susie glanced around the crowded restaurant.

It was buzzing with cool people. The bar area was busy and the restaurant, which was off to one side, a marvel of glass, chrome and plants, was likewise packed.

Couples and groups were everywhere…except at the back… Sitting at the best table in the place was…*a guy*…

For a few seconds her heart actually flipped over, because she had never seen anyone quite so stunningly good-looking in her life before. Raven-black hair, bronzed skin that spoke of some sort of exotically foreign gene pool, perfectly chiselled features… When the Big Guy above had been dishing out looks he had been first in the queue.

He was sitting in front of his laptop, oblivious to everyone around him. The sheer *cheek* of having a laptop on the table in one of the most sought-after restaurants in the city was impressive. As was the fact that he wasn't dressed for show. He was in a pair of dark jeans and a long-sleeved faded black jumper that fitted him in a way that revealed a lean, muscular body. Everything about him suggested that he didn't care where he was or who was looking at him, and there was an invisible exclusion zone around him that implied that no one should dare get too close.

He was just the sort of guy she *should* have found, scrolling through all those possibilities on the dating website—although, that said, he was probably just the sort of guy who had probably never heard of a dating website. Why would he?

And he was on his own.

The table wasn't set for two. There was a drink in front of him but he had shoved his plate and all the cutlery to one side. She was sure that there was some kind of unwritten rule about doing something like that in a place like this but he was pulling it off.

Taking a deep breath, she turned to the *maître d'*, who had swooped down to ask her whether she had reservation and said airily, 'I'm with…'

She pointed to the stranger at the back of the room and tried to smile knowingly. She had never done anything like this in her life before. But faced with the horror of date number four, the certainty of being spotted, the necessity to stay put until it was safe to slink to the table she had reserved and sample the food…desperation had made her act out of character.

'Señor Burzi…?'

'Absolutely!' If only she could scuttle back to the apartment in her glad rags to sit in front of the telly with a chocolate bar and a glass of wine. Right now that would have been heaven.

But she couldn't—and right now she didn't want to think anyway. She just didn't want to spend another evening on her own, dealing with what her parents and her sister had been telling her for the past three years…that she had to 'get some direction' in her life…that she should start thinking about a career instead of painting pictures and drawing cartoon characters…that she was *'so lucky'* to have been given the education that she had and that she owed it to herself to make the best of it… Perhaps they weren't quite so brutally honest, but she could read between the lines.

'Is Señor Burzi expecting you, Miss…?'

'Of course he is! I wouldn't be asking to join him if he wasn't, would I?'

She began walking purposefully over to the dark, sexy stranger, hoping and praying that her date wouldn't spot her, and hoping and praying even more that the *maître d'* wouldn't create an embarrassing fuss and chuck her out.

Head down, she practically collided with the table, and was aware of two piercing dark eyes shifting from the computer to her flushed face as she plopped down in one of the empty chairs.

'What the hell…? Who the hell are *you*?'

'Señor Burzi…this lady said that she was expecting to join you…'

'I'm really sorry. I know I'm probably interrupting you. But, please…could you just bear with me for a few minutes? I…I'm in a bit of a sticky situation…'

'Show her out, Giorgio, and next time please don't make the mistake of bringing anyone to my table unless I tell you to.'

His voice was deep and dark and velvety and perfectly matched the way he looked. His attention had returned to whatever was on his computer. She was dismissed. She would be chucked out of the restaurant.

Panic filled her. Panic and just…just a feeling of hopelessness. She should never have been persuaded by her two best friends into this crazy online dating situation. The thought of being escorted out of the restaurant like a common criminal, while everyone including her yellow-jumpered date turned and stared and sniggered, was just too much.

'Just a few minutes. I just need somewhere to…er…sit for a few minutes…'

This time the man did look up, and she had to force herself not to stare because up close he was even better looking than he had appeared from a distance. His eyes were navy blue and he had eyelashes to die for—long, thick and dark, and right now fringing eyes that were the temperature of ice.

'Not my problem. And how the hell did you find out that I was going to be here?' he asked coldly. He spared a glance for the *maître d'*, who was hovering and wringing his hands. 'Leave us, Giorgio. I'll get rid of her myself.'

'Sorry?' Susie looked at him blankly.

'I haven't got time for this. I have no idea how you found out where I was, but now that you're here let me make myself perfectly clear. Whatever begging mission you're on, you can forget it. Charitable donations are handled by my company. Donations of any other nature are not on the table. And a word to the wise…? Next time you get it into your head to start digging for gold, try being a little more subtle. Now, I'm giving you the option of making a dignified exit or being thrown out. Which one would you rather go for?'

Angry colour had seeped into her cheeks as the meaning of what he was saying gradually became clear.

She had no idea who the man was, but he actually thought that she had *targeted* him! Thought that she was making a play for him because she wanted to ask him for *money*!

'Are you accusing me of coming here to ask you for money?'

The man gave a bark of humourless laughter and raked his eyes over her. 'Clever deduction. Now, what's your choice of exit going to be?'

'I didn't come here to ask for money. I don't even know who you are…'

'Now, I wonder why I find that hard to believe?'

'Please—just hear me out. I honestly don't make it a habit to approach strange men in…er…bars…or even expensive restaurants…but I won't be long…'

She had as much right to be here as he did. Admittedly not actually *at his table*, but in the restaurant…generally speaking.

She actually had her own table booked, and would be forking out for some very expensive food just as soon as her blind date left and she could relax—and that was more than could be said for him, judging from the way his plate had been shoved to one side. One drink wasn't going to make the restaurant owner a rich guy, was it? In fact he was *just* the sort of customer a restaurant owner would hate! The sort of customer who booked a table, had a drink, made it last for four hours and refused to budge for the remainder of the evening.

'I haven't come here because I'm targeting you for money,' she repeated urgently, leaning forward, elbows resting on the table. 'And, by the way, I feel *very sorry for you* if you can't talk to a stranger for three minutes without thinking that they're going to ask you to put your hand in your pocket and write them out a cheque! You're the only person in this place on your own and I...I...just need to kill a little time before I'm shown to my table. I do have, actually, a valid reservation. And I will be eating.'

She took a deep breath and powered on before he had a chance to throw her out on her ear—because, whether she had a valid reason to be there or not, she certainly didn't have a valid reason to gatecrash his table.

'Do you see the guy sitting at the bar?'

Humiliation made her skin prickle. She had always been a people person. Finding herself stared at as though she was something that had crawled in off the streets—something that needed to be bagged and binned immediately—was a new experience for her and she didn't like it.

His icy silence squashed her natural breeziness like a pin being stuck into a balloon.

Sergio Burzi was frankly incredulous. Had she just told him that she *felt sorry for him* or had he misheard? He felt as though he had been run over by a bus, and was momentarily too dazed to do anything but pick himself up and dust himself down.

'There are a lot of guys at the bar,' he said.

So she would eventually do one of two things. Ask outright for money for some hare-brained scheme or else try and cosy up to him. He was a target for gold-diggers, and gold-diggers came in all different shapes and sizes and plied their trade with the back-up of all sorts of sob stories and fairytales.

But he was between women...jaded with the opposite sex. He liked them clever, career-orientated...he liked women who had purposeful, goal-orientated lives, who weren't clingy and emotional. He had had them by the bucketload, but recently...they did less and less for him. Not even the chase was as stimulating as it had used to be, and more often than not the 'catch of the day' became boring in a matter of weeks.

What was the harm in letting this woman sit with him for a couple of minutes before he got rid of her?

She was putting on a damn fine show and she was really rather attractive. Big brown eyes, blonde curly hair that looked as though it had only a passing acquaintance with a brush, full, sexy lips...

A sharp pang of pure lust hit him deep in the gut. He had a vivid image of how that cloud of strawberry blonde hair would look spread across his pillow, her pale skin against his much darker bronze.

It just showed how neglected his sex-life had been of late. He had dispatched his last girlfriend over two months ago and hadn't had the energy or the desire to replace her.

And now this tawdry little gold-digger had stirred him up. He sat back, easing the discomfort of a sudden rock-hard erection, and gave her his undivided attention.

'Which one are you talking about?' he asked, angling his big body so that he could extend his long legs to one side. 'And why should I be looking at him?'

Susie relaxed fractionally. He was prepared to listen to what she had to say. This would be the end of her learning curve. No more blind dates. *Ever.*

'Yellow jumper. Mustard trousers. Thin sandy hair. Do you see him?'

Sergio glanced at the bar and then back to her flushed, earnest face. 'I see him.'

He was beginning to enjoy himself. He could see Giorgio out of the corner of his eye, anxiously watching the table, ready to spring into action should he need to, and Sergio gave just the slightest shake of his head.

She was going round the houses to get to the point, but

she had managed to pique his interest. That in itself was worth the storyline.

When she finally made a move on him he wondered whether he would take her up on the offer... She wasn't his type, but wasn't a change as good as a rest?

'And you've pointed him out to me because...?'

'He's my blind date and I'm trying to avoid him.'

She groaned, looked at the man sitting opposite her, and her breathing picked up because those lazy, dark, fathomless eyes made her nervous and excited at the same time... gave her a weird, giddy feeling.

'I met him on one of those dating websites,' she confided glumly. 'They cater for the under-thirties. You know the kind of thing...young people seeking serious relationships... It's a lie. None of them are. I feel awful about standing up poor Phil, but I just can't face another date frantically trying to make small talk while the minutes tick by at a snail's pace...'

Sergio wondered what she would do if he called her bluff by going across to Mr Yellow Jumper and asking whether he was there to meet someone from a dating agency.

'I guess he's panicking because I've stood him up. I'd hate someone to stand *me* up. But, like I said, I just can't face all that silly, pointless conversation...'

'He doesn't appear to be overly heartbroken. In fact he seems to be chatting up an older woman at the bar.'

'What?'

'Blonde hair...smartly dressed... Yes, they appear to be leaving...together...' *Maybe because she was his original date...*

'I don't believe it! Didn't I tell you?' Susie said bitterly. 'Serious relationships... *Ha!* One-night stand relationships, more like it.'

She might not have wanted to go through with the ordeal but she was insulted that she had been dumped without even being interviewed for the job.

'Online dating isn't what it's cracked up to be. Forget about all those pictures of starry-eyed couples gazing lovingly at one another over a romantic meal, or dashing along a beach grinning like star-struck maniacs and holding hands. It's all just advertising. Just look at *my* date. He couldn't even hang around and wait a few minutes for me to show up.'

'I thought you were trying to avoid him?'

'That's not the point. The point is that he could have hung around a bit longer before making off with the first available woman who gave him the time of day!'

Susie wouldn't have dreamt of finding her perfect guy via a computer—except for the fact that The Big Wedding was getting closer, and she couldn't face showing up without any boyfriend in tow or, worse, with one of her arty, creative crowd who would be politely dismissed as yet another loser because 'poor little Susie' just didn't seem to have what it took to find herself a halfway decent boyfriend.

Poor little Susie can't even get her love-life in order...

She knew she shouldn't care, but the big Three-Oh was only five years away and she suddenly and inexplicably felt that her time was running out. Surely it wasn't asking too much for *one* part of her life to be sorted out?

'I'll make sure to steer clear of dating sites on the internet. Why don't you have a glass of wine and take your coat off, by the way?'

'There's no need to keep chatting to me, Mr... Sorry, I've completely forgotten your name...'

'You can call me Sergio. And you are...?'

'Susie.'

She politely held out her hand and the warmth of his long fingers as he clasped it sent a jolt of electricity racing through her body, as though she had suddenly been plugged into a light socket. She almost wanted to rub her hand on her dress when it was released.

'And I'll leave you to get on with…er…what you were doing…'

Sergio toyed with the idea of calling her bluff and then decided against it. He hadn't been this engaged for a while. The work that was waiting to be done could take a back seat.

He waved at his computer without taking his eyes from her face. 'What does it look like I was doing?'

'I know. Pretty dull. Work. I don't know how you can concentrate in a place like this. I'd be too busy looking around and people-watching.' She made a sympathetic face and began to stand up.

'Sit.'

Sergio had made his mind up. So what if she was a gold-digger? She would discover soon enough that she had chosen the wrong place to go prospecting, but he was enjoying her company. He was certainly enjoying what she was doing to his body.

Susie frowned and hesitated. 'Do you usually order people around?'

'It comes naturally,' he said, with a sudden smile that shook her to the core. 'Arrogance is apparently one of my many faults…'

'And you have a lot, do you? Faults, I mean…?'

'Too many to mention. Now, you came here to eat and drink. Sit. Please. Allow me to replace your erstwhile date for the evening…'

He almost burst out laughing at the irony of his pretending to believe the little white lies she had told him but, hell, she was the most creative and amusing woman he had met in a long time.

Susie was charmed. Not only was he drop-dead gorgeous, but how many men admitted to having failings? Most of them were far too busy Photoshopping their pictures, slashing twenty years off their real age and pretending that they weren't five foot two.

And wasn't he now inviting her to have dinner with him?

'Why don't you join *me?* My table is…'

She looked around for an empty table and sighed because it had probably been taken. Arriving late would *not* be an option for anyone who had booked a table in this place. There would be a long list of people waiting in the wings for tables booked by poor, hapless idiots who might have run into delays on the Underground or got snagged in traffic on the way.

'Where…?' Sergio made a show of trying to spot a vacant table.

'Gone.' She sighed again.

'Oh, dear.'

'I don't normally do…*this*…' she began, although a little thrill darted through her at the thought of having dinner with him.

He was so unlike any man she had ever met. Her last boyfriend, Aidan, had been a would-be writer who went on protest rallies, railed against 'capitalist pigs' and had now disappeared to the other side of the world, where he was bumming around in search of ideas for his next book, doing little jobs to keep himself going. They vaguely kept in touch.

'Do what?' Sergio inclined his head to one side.

'Force myself on strangers and then accept meals from them. I'll join you on one condition, and it's that I pay for myself… I'd offer to pay for you as well, but I'm not in a great place financially at the moment…'

And she wouldn't be there at all were it not for her parents' generosity. She had always made it a point to go it on her own, but the temptation to have a free meal at the hottest ticket in town had been irresistible.

'By which you mean…?' Sergio signalled to a waiter for menus and then relaxed back, prepared to be amused.

'I'm between jobs, in actual fact. Well, no, that's not *strictly* true. I'm a freelance artist, but still quite new to the business. I haven't had time to make many contacts so jobs are pretty thin on the ground at the moment. Things will pick up. I'm pretty sure of that. But it's difficult breaking through… I make ends meet working at a pub near to where I live. I can only hope that I get some work soon— perhaps a long-term contract, which would be brilliant. Via word of mouth… Of course I've been in touch with every pu—'

'Enough. Really not all that interested in the backstory. Correct me if I'm wrong, but the bottom line is that you're broke because you can't find regular work?'

'It's a competitive world out there when it comes to graphic art and illustrations…'

'Indeed.'

'I did a secretarial course when I left school…I had a few jobs doing secretarial work, but I didn't enjoy it.'

'Expensive choice of restaurant for someone who happens to be currently financially challenged.'

But then that wouldn't be a consideration, bearing in mind she would have known, if she played her cards right that he would pick up the tab—and if not him, then any other lone punter. This wasn't a place frequented by paupers. She was sex on legs and that worked nine times out of ten.

Susie opened her mouth to tell him that, actually, her parents would be the ones picking up the tab and promptly closed it—because how pathetic was that? She was twenty-five years old and still reliant on handouts from her parents for the occasional treat. Shame washed over her.

'Sometimes…ah…you just have to splash out now and again…' she countered feebly.

'Maybe your online date would have done the gentlemanly thing and treated you to the meal,' Sergio humoured her, 'had he only stayed the course…'

'I doubt that. Anyway, I wouldn't have allowed him to do that. The last thing I would have wanted would have been to give him any ideas.'

'Any ideas…?'

'That if he paid for my meal he got me thrown in as an added extra…'

She reddened as Sergio looked at her with raised eyebrows.

'And if *I* pay for your meal do you think that *I* might see you as dessert?' he murmured.

All at once her head was full of images of him having her as his dessert…taking her to his bed, making love with her, touching and tasting her everywhere…

And the way he was looking at her…

It sent thrilling little shivers up and down her spine. His navy eyes were cool, speculative… She was a tasty little morsel and he was idly contemplating the pros and cons of sampling her…

That was what it felt like and, yes, it should have had her bristling with indignation but…it didn't.

She licked her lips nervously—an unconsciously erotic little gesture that made Sergio shift in his chair, easing the pain of an erection that wasn't going anywhere.

'The coat,' he reminded her softly. 'Take it off.'

Susie obeyed. She got the feeling that people always obeyed what he said. Maybe that was why he was allowed to take up valuable space in a pricey restaurant without actually putting any money in the coffers by eating. She had thought he was being charming and self-deprecating when he had described himself as arrogant. Maybe he was just being truthful.

The coat came off.

Sergio's breath caught in his throat. What had he been expecting? He didn't know. He just knew that if she was out to see what she could get from him, then she had been inspired in her choice of dress, because it displayed every inch of her fabulous figure in loving detail. The tiny waist. The generous breasts. Shapely legs. But she wasn't overly tall, and he liked tall. She wasn't brunette, and he preferred brunettes. And she certainly wasn't a career woman— unless you could call not having a steady job a career choice—and career women were the only women who interested him.

But she was doing terrific things to his libido.

He smiled a slow, curling smile as he inspected her lazily from head to toe and back again.

'That's rude!' Hot and bothered, Susie hurriedly sat down and wiped clammy hands on the dress.

'Come again?'

'That's *rude*…'

'Don't tell me you don't like being looked at? If you didn't you wouldn't be wearing a red dress that leaves very little to the imagination.'

'It was a mistake buy.'

She was mortified to feel dampness seeping through her underwear and the tingle of her nipples, which had reacted to that lingering, unhurried inspection as though they were being played with.

What was going on? she wondered in confusion. She never reacted to guys like this. She was comfortable around them. Always had been. Yes, she had had two boyfriends, but neither of them had had this sort of effect on her.

Mistake buy? Sergio nearly burst out laughing. 'Mistake buys' weren't small, red and sexy. Small, red and sexy were designed to do one thing and one thing only, and that was to attract a man. To attract, in this case, *him*. It had worked. He was attracted.

And the way she could barely meet his eyes... She was the very picture of flustered, pink-cheeked innocence. It might be great acting, but the flustered pink-cheeked innocence was as sexy as the dress.

Hats off to her for a new and interesting route to getting through to him. Had she just turned up at the bar wearing the sexy red dress he might have looked but he wouldn't have gone there. But her storyline... She had enticed him with more than the dress and the body...she had enticed him with her personality—and, frankly, he was in the mood to be enticed.

She was a refreshing change. He needed a break from intellectual women who had opinions and could become borderline tedious on the subject of their high-powered careers. What could be more of a break than a frisky little number who didn't have a job?

'I'd dispute that,' he told her, with that same curling smile that made her short of breath. 'In fact, from where I'm sitting, it looks like anything *but* a mistake buy.'

He was hardly aware of their glasses being refilled by a waiter, or of menus being placed in front of them. In fact he was hardly aware of ordering food.

'So, does the bartending and the occasional picture-painting pay the rent? In London?' he asked.

'Just about. I can't say I have much left over at the end of the month…'

Her parents would have loved nothing more than to install her in their grand apartment in Kensington, which was only used when they occasionally decided to descend on the city for the theatre or the opera, but she had always stuck to her guns and refused the offer.

Pride, however, *did* entail roughing it in a not particularly great part of London and having to put up with a good-natured but lazy landlord who didn't see a problem with eccentric central heating and appliances that only worked when they felt like it.

'And yet you're here…?'

'Sometimes you've just got to live a little.' Susie blushed and looked away. 'I should have done what I always wanted to do,' she said, staring off into the distance. 'I mean, have *you* ever found yourself sucked into following a career path that just wasn't for you?'

She had been eighteen…with no interest in going to university…and the family consensus had been that a secretarial career would at least provide a steady income, with the possibility of branching out at a future date. The unspoken conclusion had been that she was just not academic enough for much else.

'No.'

'You mean you've *always* known what you wanted to do with your life? Where you wanted to go and how to get there?'

'Circumstances have a cunning way of steering us down an inevitable road,' Sergio murmured, a little surprised to be participating in this abstract conversation.

'What does that mean?'

'So you were "sucked into" becoming a secretary…?'

Susie duly noted his avoidance of her question—and yet

he had sounded, just then, as though he had been speaking from experience...*what* experience?

'It seemed to make sense at the time.' And anything that made sense had seemed so important at the time—more important than standing her ground and pursuing a career in fine art.

'But in retrospect it was the biggest mistake of your life, because things that are done because they make sense are not always the things one ends up enjoying...?'

'That's *so true*!' Susie leaned forward. She laughed, delighted that he had caught on so quickly, had almost read her mind and expressed her thoughts in a handful of words. 'You're very insightful,' she murmured shyly.

Sergio raised his eyebrows. Insightful? One adjective that had never before been applied to him.

'I wouldn't get carried away,' he murmured drily. 'If I were you I'd remember what I told you before. I'm arrogant...you'd be far better off bearing that in mind...'

CHAPTER TWO

NATURALLY SUSIE OFFERED to pay her half.

'I insist,' she told him firmly. 'I dumped myself on you. The last thing I want is for you to find yourself having to buy dinner for me. And a very expensive dinner as well.'

'I don't do anything in life because I *have* to,' Sergio informed her. 'At any rate, I don't pay when I come here.'

'You *don't pay*? What does *that* mean?'

'I have an understanding here…' So she knew he was rich? That wasn't too difficult. He was well known—if not because he appeared so often in the financial pages, then because he appeared with equal regularity in the gossip columns of tabloids. Whether she knew what, precisely, he owned, he had no idea—and who cared?

He had already made his mind up.

Maybe he had made it up the second his libido had been galvanised into unexpected reaction.

She had come looking for fun and cash. She was heading in the right direction for fun…

And the cash? He was a generous lover, so who knew? If she was looking for something more significant…if she was in search of involvement on an emotional level…then of course she would be in for a rude awakening. But for the moment he liked the thought of taking her to his bed…removing that provocative little red number inch by gradual inch…and then exploring the body underneath also inch by gradual inch…

'How can you have an "understanding" with a restaurant?' Susie asked dubiously. 'Unless… Are you related to the owner? Or does the owner owe you a favour…?' She frowned and chewed her lip anxiously. 'You're not…not connected to the Mafia, are you?'

For a few seconds Sergio thought he had misheard her, but she was still staring at him, her almond-shaped brown eyes wary.

'Have you actually just asked me whether I was connected to the *Mafia*…?' Incredulity almost deprived him of the power of speech. No one, *but no one,* had ever dared go this far…

In fact no one, and certainly no woman, had ever dared challenge him in *any* way.

Maybe because they knew instinctively that he wasn't into verbal challenges. Some women might think it a turn-on to needle him. The few who had thought so had learned pretty damn quickly that it wasn't.

He was almost more incredulous that the woman appeared actually to be waiting for an answer!

'Well?' she asked, proving him right. 'You haven't answered.'

'No! I am categorically *not* related to the Mafia!'

'That's good.'

'Because…?'

'No reason.' Susie shrugged and realised with a little jolt of horror that she had actually begun to hope that she'd see him again. Begun to hope all sorts of things!

'Come on…'

Sergio stood up and she instantly followed suit, glaringly conscious of what she was wearing now that she was no longer sitting down.

She slipped the black cape on and when she reached to tighten it around her he rested his hand briefly over hers.

That electric charge again—that hot, fierce current running through her that made her heart skip a beat and the breath catch painfully in her throat.

'Come on…?' she parroted weakly. 'Come on…where?'

Sergio stood next to her, looking down at her upturned heart-shaped face. So many times she should have turned him off completely—starting with her crazy urge to confide and ending with her even crazier notion that he was some kind of gangster…

Yet was he turned off? *No.* He was a born predator, and he was a little relieved to find all those instincts alive and kicking, having been dormant for way too long for a man like him.

'A number of choices here…' Sergio murmured, enjoying the hectic colour in her cheeks and marvelling that she could marshal her expression into exactly the one she wanted to have on show.

'Really?' Susie squeaked, obediently falling in line with him as he headed out, oblivious to the covert stares following him and certainly oblivious to whoever was responsible for supplying him with free food—whoever he had his so-called 'understanding' with… Maybe the *maître d'*, who had not reappeared but who had been visible out of the corner of her eye, keeping a watchful nervous eye on their table.

Just in case, Susie thought, she outstayed her welcome and needed to be flung out urgently and without delay.

'Option one…' He pulled out his mobile, quickly texted, flipped it shut. On cue, a long, sleek black car appeared out of nowhere. He held open the passenger door for her and she hesitated—because he was, after all, a complete stranger.

Maybe not a member of the Mafia, but still a stranger! She wouldn't have dreamt of getting in a car with anyone she'd met online dating, so why was she now contemplating it?

'Option one is that we move on from here to somewhere else. I'm a member of an exclusive club in Knightsbridge. They do an excellent selection of after-dinner liqueurs.'

'I can't get into this car with you…' She eyed the luxurious interior with unhealthy longing.

He had a chauffeur. There was someone at the wheel. It wouldn't *actually* be just the two of them…

'Option two is that we just head back to my place and cut through the middleman. A twenty-minute drive at this time of night. The views from my apartment would astound you.'

Susie gulped. 'And—and option three…?' she stammered, no closer to sliding into the back seat of the car and yet no nearer to fleeing the scene either.

'The third option is that you scamper away and you never see me again.'

He leaned indolently against the open door, everything about his body language unhurried.

He wouldn't try to stop her if she bolted for the nearest bus. In fact she could almost hear him chuckling under his breath if she chose option three—just as she could still hear him telling her that the things you did because they made sense weren't always the things you ended up enjoying.

This dark, impossibly sexy, impossibly articulate, impossibly self-assured man was out of her league. She wasn't the sort of sophisticated, self-confident academic like her sister, who could attract men like him. It just didn't make any sense.

But neither had that fine art course she had wanted to do… The secretarial course had made sense, and a fat lot of good *that* had done her in the long run. She had still ended up digging her heels in and doing what she should have done in the first place—except she was now older as she started the climb up the career ladder.

She tightened her coat around her, her heart beating madly. It was cold out here—one of those freezing, sleety January evenings that put a depressing spin on everything. People swarmed around them, some turning to glance back over their shoulders.

'We could talk…I guess…'

Sergio smiled. Had he doubted that she would take him up on his offer? Not really. He had sensed that charge between them, invisible but so tangible he could almost have reached out and clasped it in the palm of his hand.

'We could—although I've often found that there are far more interesting things to do with a woman than talk. Now, are you going to get in?'

Susie hopped in, breathing in the smell of expensive leather and feeling the warmth of the car wrap around her. She shifted over to the window, still not entirely sure what had propelled her into doing something as extraordinary as climbing into a car with a guy she'd known for all of five minutes.

'Club or my place?'

Sergio turned to her and all at once she felt the intimacy between them like a force.

His beautiful face was all shadows and dark, brooding angles. God, she could stare at this man and keep staring. The cute guys she had met in the past seemed like inept little boys in comparison. Actually, they probably were. This was a powerful alpha male, the leader of the pack, the king of the jungle, and a shiver of unbridled excitement rippled through her.

'Well…'

She let that one syllable drag out and for Sergio that was answer in itself. He leaned forward and told his driver to head home, and then he relaxed back, sprawled against the car door and looked at her.

He liked this game she was playing. How many men had she approached in the past? he wondered. How many stories did she have up her sleeve? That hesitant, glorious air of innocence could go a long way...

'So if you didn't like secretarial work,' he said obligingly, very happy to chat to her about the past she probably altered according to her audience, 'why did you go in for it in the first place?'

'What do *you* do?' Susie asked curiously, as always reluctant to point out all her deficiencies—at least as compared to her gifted family members. Especially to this man who, for reasons unknown, she was driven to try and impress.

Sergio threw her an amused, vaguely disbelieving look and she stared back at him and laughed.

It was an infectious laugh. It was the laugh of someone who enjoyed laughing. His own lips twitched.

'Share the joke?' he drawled drily.

'You think I know who you are, don't you? I bet you still think I'm after whatever money you have —even though I've told you that I'm not.'

'You surely must have heard of me?' Sergio heard himself say.

Her laughter subsided into a grin. 'Why?'

'Because my name crops up regularly. I'm either making money or giving it away.'

'What does *that* mean?'

The undercurrent threading through their conversation felt dangerous, heady and compelling. The way those deep, penetrating eyes roved over her made her feel hot and breathless, and she had never enjoyed a sensation more in her life.

'It means I make money—and lots of it.'

'Doing what?'

'All sorts of things,' Sergio said with a shrug. 'I buy things, take things over, invest in things, build things… I own the restaurant, as a matter of fact. It's one of five scattered across the country that specialise in superb food and an edgy atmosphere.'

'You *own* that restaurant?'

Her mouth fell open and Sergio couldn't help himself. He laughed.

'Are you telling me you weren't aware of that?'

'Why should I be?' She looked at him, bemused. 'I honestly had no idea,' she told him. 'And if you really and truly believe that I only went there to try and get your attention because you're rich, then you can ask your driver to stop and I'll get out and find my own way back home.'

'You don't mean that.'

She didn't answer. Instead she rapped on the glass partition separating them from his driver. He caught her wrist and held on to it until she reluctantly met his eyes.

'You headed straight over to my table,' he said grimly. 'You sat down uninvited until you managed to wangle dinner, and now here you are, in my car, heading back to my place… What's a billionaire supposed to think?'

Susie yanked her hand away, stung, because what he said might make sense on the surface but was so far from the truth that it was laughable.

Sergio noted the glimmer of tears glazing her eyes and for a few seconds had some doubts about the conclusions he had drawn. She had squeezed herself tightly against the car door and he had the impression that if she could have made herself disappear in a puff of smoke she would have.

'Well?' he persisted roughly. 'What *am* I supposed to think?'

'You're supposed to believe what I've told you.'

He laughed humourlessly. 'Women have an unfortunate habit of acting out of character the second they're exposed to a man with a lot of money.'

'Do they? I wouldn't know. I want to get out. I want to go home. I should never have agreed to get in this car with you in the first place. You think I've only done it because I'm after your money and you don't want to believe me when I tell you that you're wrong. Well, how do I know that you're an honourable guy? How do I know that you're not going to take me back to your place and...and...?'

'Don't even *think* of going there!'

Sergio was genuinely outraged that she could believe the worst of him but he grudgingly recognised the irony of the situation. He wasn't prepared to believe a word of what she was saying so why should *she* believe a word of what *he* was telling her? He clearly had money, but that didn't mean he was...*an honourable guy*...

He vaguely wondered what she'd meant by that anyway.

'I don't need to force myself on women,' he said flatly.

Susie could believe that. He had a point. 'So if I told you that I wanted to get out—right here, right now...?'

'I wouldn't try and stop you.'

He raked impatient fingers through his dark hair and shot her a fulminating look from under his lashes. Had he *ever* had so much conversation with any woman before getting into bed with her? Sure, he might discuss the state of the world, what was happening in the news, politics... The women he dated always enjoyed displaying the length, breadth and width of their intellect...

But *feelings*...?

He met her stubborn stare and sighed. 'Why were you

trying to find a man through the internet? Hasn't anyone ever told you that it's not safe?'

Susie relaxed. He had meant it when he had told her that he would drop her off if she asked. She had seen it in his eyes. And she believed him when he said that he had no need to force himself on a woman. She imagined his danger was in trying to escape women forcing themselves on *him*.

He might be suspicious and downright offensive, but he was up front. And so, *so* exciting.

'Have you *any* idea how hard it is, finding a date in London? When you don't do the clubbing scene and don't have a fancy, high-powered job where there are loads of unattached eligible males?'

'No.'

'*Hard.* I mean, I *know* a lot of guys, but my friends tend to be…well…' She frowned. 'They're creative types. A couple of graphic designers who freelance… One makes amazing designs for wallpapers…three work in publishing…'

'And eligible men?' Sergio asked, moving the conversation along, curious in spite of himself.

'Lots of men—but none of them are what you might call "eligible". To be honest, quite a few of the guys I know are gay…so when one of my friends suggested I see what was out there on the internet, I didn't think it was such a bad idea. Besides…'

She talked a lot, but strangely he didn't seem to mind. He wondered whether it was the lingering effect of the red dress. Or the novelty of someone who didn't see it as her duty to show him how bright she was and how many degrees she had obtained to get where she had. Or the way her blonde hair spilled over her shoulders in unruly curls.

'Besides…?' he inserted encouragingly.

'I have a wedding coming up.'

Sergio could smell a convoluted story in the making. For the moment, however, his initial suspicions about her were on the back burner. He hadn't discarded them completely, but he wasn't going to allow them to dictate the outcome of this very, very unusual encounter.

'I'm boring you, aren't I?'

'On the contrary. You're taking me down all sorts of roads I've never travelled before.'

'Am I?' Susie wasn't sure whether she should be flattered by that or offended. She hesitated, distracted by what he had said. 'What sort of roads do you normally go down with…er…women…?'

Sergio spread his hands wide and shot her a rueful, amused smile that did all those wonderful tingly things to her body. 'The women I date are almost exclusively career women…'

'Oh. Right. I see.' Disappointment bit into her because it made sense. He was rich and he was smart. Of *course* he would be attracted to smart and probably rich women. Like always attracted like, didn't it? 'Career women…'

'Big jobs…daily decision-making that in some cases can affect the lives of the people around them…packed agendas and hectic schedules…'

Saying it aloud made him wonder what he saw in those types, but that was just a fleeting thought because he knew exactly what he saw in them—just as he knew exactly the sort of women he had programmed himself to avoid like the plague.

Dominique Duval.

It was a name that didn't often spring to mind. He had ruthlessly and successfully eliminated it from conscious thought. But vocalising the sort of women he dated had thrown up the comparison and his lips thinned with in-

stant distaste. The past might be buried deep but it was
never truly forgotten, was it?

'What's the matter?' Susie leaned forward, startled
by his darkening expression and immediately jumping
to the conclusion that she was somehow responsible for
it. And then almost as quickly she got annoyed, because
she hadn't said anything that could remotely be construed
as offensive.

When it came to being offensive he was the one win-
ning the race!

'Just thinking back to a very significant person in
my life.' Sergio's voice was cold and hard. 'A delightful
woman who has ensured that when it comes to any sort
of involvement with the opposite sex I always make sure
to steer clear of types like *her*. Learning curves...' He
was smiling again, the tightness around his mouth gone
although his eyes were still cool. 'I like to pay attention
to them...'

'Me too.'

Susie didn't know what had just happened there. What
she *did* know was that she wasn't going to go down Confidence Lane and start telling him all about *her* family and
her learning curves.

She was already reaching the conclusion that the only
reason he had even glanced in her direction was because
of her novelty value. If he only dated clever career women,
someone plonking herself at his table with a long-winded
tale of online dating mishaps would have been a shock to
the system.

So who *was* this woman who had shaped his responses
to the opposite sex and determined the sort of women he
chose to date? She assumed some past love affair. Maybe
he had fallen in love with the wrong girl? The fact that he
had taken it so badly—badly enough to change the way

he looked at his relationships—was telling. He had fallen in love and got burned.

Her thoughts rambled on until she surfaced to hear him asking her about the wedding she had mentioned.

'Wedding?' She gave an airy laugh and flapped her hand in a dismissive gesture. 'What wedding?'

'The one you have coming up... You were about to launch into a tale of young love and confetti...'

'Wow. You live *here?* Isn't this the most expensive place to live on the planet?' She craned forward, squinting into the darkness and staring up and up and up at the spire of glass rising into the clouds.

As a diversion from a conversation she no longer wanted to have, it worked.

The apartment her parents owned was nice. No, it was better than *nice.* It was in a great location, and had been refurbished to a high standard, but this was the stuff of dreams—a place ordinary mortals never got to see.

She had genuinely forgotten the 'wedding on the horizon' conversation.

'Impressed?' Sergio was exiting the car and swinging round to open the passenger door for her, but she had already hopped out and was staring.

'*Very* impressed,' she confessed.

That came as no big surprise to Sergio. He imagined her place as somewhere small and damp and in poor condition, languishing in a fairly unsavoury location. Possibly directly under a flight path.

It had begun to rain—a fine, dreary drizzle. It was after ten on a dark, wintry night but there was the alluring promise of excitement within the walls of his massive apartment and he felt like a randy teenager at the conclusion of a first date with the hottest girl in school.

They were whooshed up to his apartment in a glass

elevator and finally, as he pushed open the door to his apartment, she managed to find her voice, which had got lost somewhere between the vast foyer and the fifteenth floor.

'This is…*incredible*—but I guess you know that already…' She laughed nervously and stared around her at a marvel of modernism. Cool abstract paintings, most of which she recognised, were hung strategically on the walls and there was an awful lot of pale marble everywhere.

She was in his apartment…

There was nothing to be nervous about. She repeated that mantra to herself as he dutifully made noises about the layout of the apartment.

So many rooms… And whilst he was obviously accustomed to the artwork, to the vast scale of everything, the avant-garde kitchen where the marble gave way to wood, the sitting area which was dominated by creams and whites… Well, she was more and more impressed with every passing step.

She peppered him with questions. Asked him how long he had lived there, if he knew his neighbours—which for some reason he found very funny—wondered aloud what would happen if he spilled red wine over the white leather sofa…

She chattered ceaselessly—because whether or not she should be nervous, *she was*.

With all her online dates—three of them, because number four had bitten the dust before they could actually meet—she had ultimately been in control. Public places, superficial conversation, awkward goodbyes…

She had not, even in passing, been tempted to go anywhere with them except to the door, where they'd parted company in different directions.

And both her relationships had started life in the friendship arena and then progressed from friendship through to curiosity and into a relationship before morphing back into friendship.

This…*was different.*

'Perhaps some coffee…?' she said.

So she was looking for a relationship? Why hide from that? He wasn't. And definitely not with someone like her. She wasn't a career woman who could talk about business stuff. That were the sort of women he dated, went out with, would consider a candidate for a relationship. He had said so himself. She was a one-off.

And he was a one-off for her as well. He was…this was…*lust.* No more, no less. Heck, she was aware of him with every fibre of her being—could feel his presence like a forbidden thrill.

So they were even. Weren't they?

Still…a cup of coffee might settle her nerves. She pictured them heading up to that split galleried landing straight to his bedroom…where he would turn to her, expecting her to launch herself into abandoned sex when in fact she might have had two boyfriends but she was woefully short on the sort of experience she figured he would be used to.

'You want…coffee…? At this hour?' Sergio leaned against the kitchen counter and looked at her evenly.

'Maybe a nightcap…' A strong dose of hard liquor would definitely steady her nerves. Or else knock her out completely. Both options were preferable to the frantic flutter in her stomach.

'Sit down,' Sergio told her gently.

He propelled her towards one of the black leather chairs at the kitchen table and then perched on the side of the table, which was a beaten metal affair the likes of which she had never seen in her life before. She stared at it fixedly and tried not to let her eyes wander to the strain of his trousers pulling taut across a muscular thigh.

'So you want either a cup of coffee or a nightcap?' he mused, tilting her face upwards so that she could look at him.

What was he to think? He didn't know. They were in his apartment and she should be coming on to him. That was how the game was played. Was this some cunning ploy to hold his interest? He didn't want to let go of his natural instinct to suspect the unexpected, but some other natural instinct inside him—one that had never surfaced before—was pushing him in a different direction.

'Either or…' Susie blinked and licked her lips.

'Do you usually have nightcaps?'

'Not usually, no…'

'Only when you go on dates?'

'I…I don't really do a lot of dating, as it happens.'

'Just random ones with strange men you meet on the internet?'

'I would never have *dreamt* of having any sort of nightcap with any of those guys I arranged to meet,' she told him truthfully. 'They were pretty awful. Well, not awful. Just…*boring and average*…'

'Is there a hidden compliment in there somewhere for me?'

'You really *are* arrogant!' But a little smile hovered on her lips and she relaxed fractionally.

'And *you're* very sexy,' Sergio told her bluntly. 'So why the hell do you think that the only way to meet a man is on the internet?'

'You think I'm sexy?'

'I think you're sexy. Beyond that, I don't know *what* to think—and, take it from me, that's a first.' He stood up and sauntered over to a complicated coffee maker. 'Now,

I'm going to make you a cup of coffee and then I'm going to get my driver to take you back to your place.'

'No!'

She would never see him again. Thrown into a state of confusion by the tumult of emotion that accompanied that thought, Susie stared at him, dry-mouthed.

Sergio ignored her outburst. He wasn't up for this—however intriguing it might be and however much it rescued him from his emotional torpor. This was a complication, and he could do without complications.

When it came to women, he liked to know what he was dealing with. He had no idea what he was dealing with here. Gold-digger? A sexy little number who wanted to press all his buttons and was doing so via a roundabout route? Or an up front and honest young girl who genuinely had no idea of her own sex appeal? And how up front and honest could she really be if she was out there, trawling the internet, advertising herself on the open market?

'Look…' Coffee made, Sergio sat next to her at the kitchen table. 'Somehow I found myself in your company tonight. *Not* what I had planned on. In fact I had planned on working, having something to eat and coming back here on my own.'

His keen eyes noted the slight tremble of her hands as she cradled the mug between them. If this was acting, then she should be up for an award.

'That said, I was more than happy with the change of plan. I have no idea who you really are, or what you really want from me, but like I said…you're sexy. And I've been celibate for two months, which is two months too long for me. But I'm not interested in going round the houses to get there. Now, drink up and I'll see you to the front door.'

'What do you mean that you have no idea who I am or what I want from you…?'

Sergio gave a sigh of pure frustration. 'I don't think I've ever talked so much with a woman before sex.'

Susie blushed and hurriedly sipped her coffee, then cleared her throat. 'You mean you just beckon a woman across, lead her to the nearest bed and…and…?'

'Oh, we *talk*…' Sergio laughed softly, enjoying the arousal that was making itself felt all over again, despite the fact that the traffic lights had turned red and he knew it was time to stop. 'High-powered career women generally have a great deal to say. It's all very civilised. We discuss the state of the world, and once that foreplay's done we head to bed.'

'Oh.'

And tonight for a while he had been caught up in the novelty of someone who *didn't* have a great deal to say on the state of the world, but he wasn't so caught up that he was going to wade through her sudden attack of nerves and hold her hand because she was suddenly feeling panicky.

He was a sophisticated man who liked sophisticated ladies but he had been willing to step out of the box for a brief session with her.

'I'd better be on my way, then.' She stood up, not looking at him. 'And I'm sorry. You know… I guess it's not really on… Well, it's *really* not on to lead a guy on. Which I wasn't doing. Actually. Because when I agreed to come here with you I thought… Well, I guess it's just not like me to have a one-night stand.' She frowned. 'In fact I've never had a one-night stand in my life before and I've never been tempted to. I don't know what came over me. Maybe it was just…walking in there and seeing Colonel Mustard at the bar… I wouldn't have approached you otherwise, you know…'

Sergio raised one hand to halt the stream of introspective conversation.

'I'm getting the picture,' he said wryly.

He ushered her out of the kitchen. He was doing the right thing. He would deal with his unwanted arousal later. In the shower. Turned to cold. That should do the trick.

'Just out of interest,' he drawled, once they were in the hall. 'if you're not the kind of girl who goes in for exciting, racy one-night stands, why the hell did you agree to this in the first place?'

He leaned against the wall and watched as she took her time fumbling with the black coat, belting it around her waist before raising her eyes to meet his.

'I don't know,' Susie admitted. 'I...I fancied you...' She went bright red and her eyes skittered away.

And that, Sergio thought, was how a guy could get insanely turned on. She could barely meet his eyes. She sounded as though the admission had been dragged out of her.

What kind of a guy would he be if he let her go away with nothing?

He moved forward, cupped his big hand behind the nape of her neck and saw her eyes widen with a mixture of surprise and hot excitement.

In that split instant he knew that he could have her if he wanted. He had never wanted anything so much in his life before, but was he going to have her? *No.* He would stick to what he knew. Safer that way. A controlled life was a life with no nasty surprises.

His mouth hovered tantalisingly close to hers and she whimpered and linked her hands around his waist. She was so wet! She eased the ache by widening her stance a little, when all she wanted was for him to put his hand there and rub away the discomfort, give her some release.

Sergio breathed in her scent, light and floral and *clean.* With a groan, he lowered his head and forgot...

everything. Her lips parted readily...her tongue flicked to meet his. He was barely aware of propelling her backwards, so that she was pressed against the wall and he was pressed against *her.* He moved against her, wanting nothing more than to rip off the black cape and hoist up the flimsy nothing of a dress. He wanted to yank her panties down and just take her...right here in the hallway...up against the wall... with her legs wrapped around him...

It took a few dazed seconds for her eyes to flutter open as he tore himself away and stood back.

'Why have you stopped?' Her nerves had gone, banished under the impact of that kiss. She hated the cooling distance he was putting between them and the fact that the bedroom beyond that short flight of stairs was no longer too scarily close for comfort.

'It's no good.' Hot blood was still pumping thick and hard in his veins. 'You're not my type.'

He should never have made a move on her—never invited her back here. But he was just so damned accustomed to having exactly what he wanted, to *taking* exactly what he wanted.

He clenched his jaw as he saw her hurt expression and told himself that this was just the sort of episode that would make her stronger. Get her off the internet for a start.

'You're either a gold-digger,' he said coolly, 'or a naive kid—and I'm not interested in either.'

'I'm not experienced enough for you...or clever enough...'

'Don't put words into my mouth. I'm telling it like it is—and here's something else... If I were you I'd think twice about trying to find your soul mate on the internet. It's a dangerous place out there...'

But not as dangerous as the inside of an exclusive restaurant in the city...

Susie knew that she shouldn't care. Okay, so she might

go away with her pride slightly dented, but he had probably done the right thing.

She drew herself up and returned his cool look with an equally cool one of her own. 'Thanks for the advice. And if *you're* glad you didn't end up in bed with me because I'm not your type, then *I'm* just as glad that I didn't end up in bed with *you* because *you're* not my type.'

She forced herself to smile…the casual, dismissive smile of one adult to another.

'And I'm not as naive as you think I am,' she lied, tossing her head. 'In fact I'm more than capable of taking care of myself *and* of having a one-night stand, if I ever want one!'

'I'm glad to hear it. Car's outside, Susie…it's been a…a highly unusual encounter…'

God, just his voice was enough to send shivers racing up and down her spine.

She held out her hand in response and pinned a smile on her face as he reached to pull open the front door. 'Thanks for dinner. And I hope you find the businesswoman of your dreams. *I'll* keep looking for the fun guy of *my* dreams…'

And she dashed out of the open door, back down in that glass lift and slap-bang outside into his chauffeur driven car. She dived in, slamming the door after her and making sure she didn't glance back as she was driven away.

CHAPTER THREE

SERGIO HAD SEEN the curiosity in the florist's eyes when he had placed his order. One hundred roses in five different colours. He could almost see the question taking shape at the back of her mind... *Who's the lucky girl?*

Stanley, his driver, was a lot more forthcoming than the florist.

'Who's the lucky girl?'

Sergio caught his driver's eye in the rear-view mirror and thought about ignoring the question.

The roses had been carefully placed in the boot, all neatly wrapped in cellophane with straw bows, their cut stems nestling in little bags of water.

'The "lucky girl" is the one you dropped home the week before last—not that it's any of your business, Stanley. In case you've forgotten the contents of your *How to Be a Good Chauffeur* manual, it's not your place to ask questions about matters that don't concern you.'

'Ah. You *must* be keen. The flowers usually only get pulled out at the *end* of one of your little flings, sir, and even so...never roses...and never that many!'

'Just drive, Stanley.'

'Nice little thing, if you don't mind me saying.'

'I'm about to make an important call, and as a matter of fact I *do* mind.'

'You'll need to be careful with that one, sir.'

Sergio gave up. He had employed Stanley for over ten years—rescued him from an inner city project that aimed to rehabilitate petty criminals and chronically out of work men back into the community by training them up in stable jobs.

It was one of the many charities sponsored by Sergio's vast conglomerate of companies.

Some of the lads went into manual labour. Working in garden centres, building sites, in restaurants... Stanley, aged twenty-eight now, once an expert car thief, had come to work for him, and their relationship had prospered against all odds.

Stanley was irreverent, outspoken, unimpressed by Sergio's trappings of wealth, and eternally grateful to have been rescued from a life of bouncing in and out of prison. He was a good lad gone bad, thanks to circumstances, and had been waiting for someone just like Sergio to get him back on the right track.

Sergio secretly enjoyed his driver's lack of due respect. He was loyal, would have lain down in front of a train for Sergio, and he knew cars like the back of his hand.

'I expect you're about to tell me why...?'

'Only if you want me to, sir. Wouldn't want to overstep my brief.'

'Spit it out, Stanley, and then focus on the road. I don't want to end up in a ditch because you're busy imparting your pearls of wisdom and not paying attention to your driving. Don't forget that your terms of employment are to drive me and not talk incessantly.'

It was not yet five in the evening, but already dark, with a fine persistent drizzle that made the pavements look slick and shiny, as though they had been covered with a fine layer of oil.

'She's not like the other women you go out with, if you don't mind me saying, sir. This one's...*different*... Don't ask me why—just a feeling I got when I was dropping her back...'

Sergio wondered whether that *feeling* would be diluted if Stanley knew the circumstances surrounding their meeting—if he knew that the *nice little thing* had shown up at his restaurant dressed to kill in a tight red dress on a supposedly mystery date with a mystery guy which may or may not have been the real reason for being there in the first place.

'But I'll leave you to get on with that important phone call now, sir. Wouldn't want you kicking me out because I'm not doing my job to Your Highness's satisfaction.'

He began to hum under his breath, leaving Sergio to get on with his thoughts.

He was being driven to Susie's house on a mission that included a hundred roses of varying colours and he didn't really know why—except that he hadn't been able to get her out of his head. He'd met the woman once, under dubious circumstances, was not convinced that she wasn't a gold-digger, had not even slept with her, and yet...

Under normal circumstances women did not intrude into his working life. They didn't show up at his office, they didn't phone him on his office line, and they never interfered with his thought processes when they weren't physically around. When he was with a woman he enjoyed her with every fibre of his being. When she wasn't around she was forgotten. It was just the way he was.

Unfortunately he had spent so much time thinking about Susie that he hadn't been able to focus. He had found himself drifting off twice during meetings, staring at his computer without really seeing the lines and columns in front of him, having to get his secretary to repeat herself on several occasions because his mind had wandered off.

He had no idea why this particular encounter had left him so distracted. It wasn't as though she was the most beautiful woman he had ever laid eyes on, nor the smartest. Her intentions were open to debate, and she had, frankly, led him up the garden path by giving off all the right signals about wanting to climb into bed with him and then, when his libido was through the roof, backing away and shooting out of his apartment like a bat out of hell.

So here he was. He didn't know what he intended to say when he showed up on her doorstep. He didn't even know if he would find her at home. Maybe she had already dry-cleaned the little red dress and was wearing it at some other rich man's hangout, on the hunt for another billionaire—someone a little less daunting.

He didn't care for the thought, and rather than spend the trip brooding consoled himself with the very pleasing prospect that if she *was* at home he would have some fun plumbing the depths of that attraction she had talked about instead of being noble and resisting what was on offer.

He'd never done that before and he'd been a fool to do it with her.

That was probably why he had found himself at the local florist and now here, in the back seat of his car. He was allergic to self-denial.

'We're here, sir.' Stanley killed the engine and met Sergio's eyes.

'She lives *here?*'

Sergio peered through the drizzle to a grim little selection of shops…a newsagent, a fish and chip takeaway, a few more that were already closed for the night and barricaded so securely that it made you wonder what sort of people lived in the neighbourhood.

'Flat above the shops, sir.'

Even grimmer. 'Should be fun, transporting the roses up to her flat,' he mused aloud. 'Who *lives* in a place like this, Stanley?'

'Several of my relatives, sir—and those would be the lucky ones.'

Sergio grunted. 'Do you know her flat number, or do we have to ring all the bells and hope for the best?'

'Flat number nine, sir. Saw her up to her front door myself.'

Susie was barely aware of her doorbell ringing until she turned down the television. The doorbell, like everything else in the tiny flat, was eccentric—sometimes working, sometimes not, and very often ringing so quietly that she had to strain her ears to hear it.

It was Friday evening and she had declined all company. Definitely no more online dating. The daring red number had been cleaned and was hanging at the back of the wardrobe as a reminder of her mistake.

Sergio Burzi.

She had looked him up on the internet—not to read what was said about him, because she wasn't that interested, but to gaze at the pictures of him…which didn't do him justice at all.

It amazed her that one random meeting with a perfect stranger had managed to throw her whole life out of kilter.

She daydreamed. She changed reality so that she had ended up spending the night with him. She wondered what it might have been like. She projected herself into a future that they would never have and fantasised about having a relationship with him—a proper relationship.

Then she remembered what he had said about the women he dated, what he had told her about the sort of women he was drawn to. Women like her sister, Alex. Clever, high-powered women, who knew what they wanted out of life the very second they emerged from the womb.

Another feeble ring from the doorbell and she padded across to the front door. Ten seconds was all it took. Her flat was so small that she could practically flick on the television in the poky sitting room while frying an egg in the kitchen.

She thought of Sergio's apartment. So vast...so modern...a stunning space where everything worked and did what it was supposed to do. The lights didn't flicker ominously, the fridge didn't stage protests against being too well stocked, the sofas didn't sag in the middle...and the bed... She could only think that his bed would be ten times the size of hers and wouldn't creak every time he moved.

Susie knew that she had to snap out of her torpor because it wouldn't get her anywhere. Her mother had telephoned the very day after her dinner with Sergio and had peppered her with questions about the new restaurant. She had been irritated when Susie had responded in monosyllables and made a great effort to try and change the conversation, having put Louise Sadler straight and told her that there had been no nice man sharing the meal with her.

Then her mother had launched into a speech about Clarissa's wedding—about how delighted everyone was that she was getting married, that it wouldn't be long before a grandchild was on the way for her mother...Louise Sadler's sister.

Susie's mother had a long-running, just below the surface competitive edge with her aunt, Kate. Two years separated them, and rumour had it that the Thornton sisters had been competing from the second her mother—the younger of the two—had uttered her first words.

Louise had married first, but Kate had had a child first.

Louise had had a job with more status, but Kate's had earned her more money.

And now Kate's daughter Clarissa was hopping up the aisle—the first in the family to do so.

Susie shuddered to think of her mother's reaction if Clarissa got pregnant and had a baby nine months after the wedding ring had been put on her finger.

It was bad enough that Alex was so involved in her fabulously important job as a neurosurgeon that there was no sign of any boyfriend on the horizon. At least in the case of her sister Louise had the 'fabulous job' to fall back on—about which she never stopped boasting.

But Susie…

No fabulous job and no boyfriend either. In fact not even any friends who were boys who could give her mother anything to brag about.

Was it any wonder that she had toyed with the idea of finding Mr Perfect via the internet? Was it any wonder that she had fallen for all those cosy pictures of loving couples and actually believed that rubbish about perfect endings?

Fighting down another wave of self-pity, she pulled open the door—to a barrage of flowers. Bunches and bunches and bunches of roses—so many roses that it had taken two people to cart them up to her flat, although she couldn't see who they were because they were shielded by the flowers.

'Sorry, you've got the wrong place.'

She moved to shut the door. Somewhere in the building some lucky girl was being bombarded with flowers, and she didn't want to be reminded of the fact that the lucky girl wasn't her.

'I would have gone more easy on the quantity if I had known that your flat was so small…'

Susie's mouth fell open. Her heart started beating so

hard that she felt giddy. The palms of her hands began to perspire. Her whole body began to perspire.

She watched as Sergio emerged from the garden centre on her doorstep.

He was as sexy as she remembered. As tall, as dark, as striking. Dark jeans clung to his lean hips and he was wearing a striped rugby jumper and loafers. It was cold outside, and she wondered how he could find a trench coat adequate cover. It was hooked over his shoulder with one finger.

'What are you doing here?'

'That will be all, Stanley.' He addressed the man next to him without taking his eyes from Susie's face.

'Why are you here?' she repeated in a dazed voice, barely aware of so many flowers being put inside her flat that she probably wouldn't be able to turn a full circle when she shut the door.

But through the daze pleasure was zinging through her—because this was one of her fantasies…the one that involved him seeking her out.

Excitement gripped her, twisting her insides and turning her legs to jelly. He was giving orders to Stanley, the really great guy who had driven her back to her flat and seen her up to her front door the previous week, in true gentleman style.

And then there were just the two of them, staring at one another, until she was knocked for six by his slow, curling smile.

He'd done the right thing.

Sergio knew that the very second the door was pulled open and he saw her again. No red dress this time. No dress at all. Baggy jogging bottoms and a grey jumper and fluffy bright pink bedroom slippers.

The sex kitten was nowhere in evidence. In her place

was a small, cute, freckle-faced, vanilla-haired girl who was gaping at him as though he had materialised out of nowhere.

And she was even sexier than he remembered.

'Are you going to ask me in?' He lounged against the door frame and continued to look at her.

'How did you find me? No, I know. Stanley knows where I live. I'm surprised he remembered the route.'

'He's talented when it comes to remembering places.'

'And maybe you'd like to tell me what the heck you're doing here?'

For a few seconds Sergio was completely thrown by that question. Automatic entry had been his expectation. Explanations to follow—not that he had really anticipated many of those. He had shown up, hadn't he? This was the first time he had ever done anything like this before, and it hadn't crossed his mind that she wouldn't be delighted with the gesture.

'Come again?'

'The last time I saw you, you told me that I was either a gold-digger or a simpleton and you weren't interested in having anything to do with me.'

'I don't believe I used the word *simpleton*.'

'As good as,' Susie retorted, her body as stiff as a plank of wood. She might have daydreamed about this, but now that he was here she couldn't just shove aside the fact that he had turned her away. 'I'm not your type…remember…?'

'I've come bearing flowers,' Sergio said incredulously, raking his fingers through his hair and wondering how such a generous gesture could garner a cross-examination.

'That still doesn't excuse what you said to me.'

But she yearned to fling open the door and let him in. Her whole body throbbed, remembering the way his lips had felt against hers, wanting more…much more.

'We can talk about this inside. Let me in. Please, Susie?'

Susie hesitated and then grudgingly stepped aside so that he could enter. As soon as he entered he seemed to fill the entire place. She busied herself gathering the flowers. She had two vases, into which she crammed as many as she could, and then she rested the remainder by the window to be sorted out later.

For the moment…

She retreated to the sofa and sat down, drawing her knees up to her chest and wrapping her arms around them.

'I admit I questioned your motives,' Sergio said heavily. He perched uncomfortably on the far end of the sofa. 'Can you blame me?'

'And what's made you change your mind.'

Sergio wasn't sure he actually *had* changed his mind, but he figured that complete honesty in this instance would be a mistake. The main thing was that she had managed to get to him in a way other women hadn't, for reasons he couldn't define, and if indeed she did turn out to be a gold-digger then she wouldn't get very far—especially as he knew what to look out for.

'I turned you away because…' He stood up and restlessly prowled through the room, subliminally clocking the fact that in between the dusty furnishings and tired decor there were one or two items of spectacular worth.

What did *that* say? What would *she* say if he pointed them out to her? How was it that she couldn't afford somewhere better to live when hanging on the wall was a tiny but extremely valuable abstract painting by an up-and-coming artist? And nestled amongst the bric-a-brac on the mantelpiece was what appeared to be an original Tiffany lamp?

His jaw tightened. Even recognising those anomalies, he still found that he was driven to stay put.

'Because…' he resumed his seat on the sagging sofa '…if you're a gold-digger then nothing's going to come of your efforts, and if you're just hopelessly naive then I was doing you a favour, because you'll end up getting hurt by me.'

Susie frowned. 'What makes you say that?'

'I don't do long-term relationships.'

'And what makes you think that I do? No, I take that back… What makes you think that I would cast *you* in the role of someone I want to have a long-term relationship with?'

'Women have a habit of becoming over-involved…'

'You're…an attractive man,' she said carefully, 'but there's no chance that I would ever become "over-involved" with someone like you…'

'Someone like me?'

'I'm a creative person…'

She thought of her parents' response to the creative types she had introduced to them in the past. Perhaps some of her friends had been a little *too* creative.

'It's not as though I would necessarily want to get involved with someone *exactly* like me…but I *would* want to get involved with someone funny, thoughtful, considerate, kind, sensitive… A guy like that would never accuse me of being a gold-digger, and he would never tell me that I'm so naive that I can't take care of myself—and he would *definitely* never be so downright arrogant as to assume that I would fall head over heels in love with him, given half a chance! I mean…who do you think you are, anyway…?'

Sergio was frankly lost for words. He wondered whether he should mention that there wasn't another woman on the planet who would react to his appearance at her front door, *carrying half a shop's worth of expensive roses*, by digging her heels in and giving him a furious lecture on all his failings.

'I came here because I felt there was unfinished business between us,' was all he could find to say.

Susie raised her eyebrows.

'Didn't you?' he asked softly. 'Feel like there was unfinished business between us?'

She hesitated.

Was that what she had been feeling?

Torn between wanting to assert her independence and show him that he couldn't just turn up at her door with a bunch of flowers and expect her to swoon and just *give in* to whatever it was that had taken her over like a virus, she was stuck for words.

'Well?' Sergio inserted smoothly, firing on all cylinders and interpreting her hesitation correctly for what it was. 'I couldn't stop thinking about you...'

He didn't make a move towards her, but he seemed able to sense every little thought running through her head with his finely tuned antennae. She had an expressive face. So much of him was tempted to give her the benefit of the doubt, to believe that she was as straightforward as she claimed to be, and yet...

Her appearance at the restaurant, the startling red dress, the ease with which she had accompanied him back to his place despite protesting that she *wasn't that sort of girl*... those random hugely expensive trinkets dotted around her flat...

'I'm not your type...' She looked at him narrowly, licked her lips. He was...formidable—lounging back there on her sofa in all his dark, dangerous, sexy glory.

'I'm willing to break the mould...'

But she didn't go in for short-lived affairs—never had. She might have broken up with her last boyfriend but it had been a relationship born from optimism that it would stay the course. Quite different from indulging in something that didn't stand a chance…

To even think about…anything at all with the man now looking at her with those midnight-blue eyes would be downright reckless.

'You told me that I wasn't your type either,' he reminded her in the same soft, speculative voice that felt like a caress. 'Maybe it's just a case of opposites attracting…'

He'd never had to work so hard with any woman before, and he wondered whether it was the irresistible lure of a challenge.

'You're not my type.'

'So why the hesitation? We can both go into this with our eyes wide open and enjoy one another or I can walk out through that door—and I promise you that there won't be a next time as far as I am concerned. This is the most I've ever had to do when it comes to chasing a woman. I've exhausted my interest in active pursuit.'

'You make it sound so…so cold…so businesslike…'

'I could wrap it up in pretty paper if you'd prefer,' Sergio said drily. 'But would that change anything? We're attracted to one another. I can feel it between us like something *alive*… And if you come a bit closer and touch me you'll certainly feel just how attracted to you I am and just how much I want to make love to you right now…'

Her heart skipped a beat. She remained where she was. He was right. There was a spark of electricity between them that crackled and there was no point denying that. And so what if he was…*practical* about whatever *this* was…? So what if he was blunt when it came to doing something about it?

The romantic in her might want to hear all the flowery stuff that came at the start of a relationship—but that flowery stuff didn't amount to very much most of the time, did it? He was giving her his own unvarnished view of what they had.

Mutual, physical attraction—take it or leave it.

'Are you so…so cold and detached with other women?' she asked. Or was he like this only with her because he'd known from the get-go that she wasn't the sort of woman who would ever be able to hold his interest for very long?

'You talk a lot…'

But he grinned and a little more of her melted. He had the most amazing grin. It altered the harsh contours of his beautiful face and made him seem suddenly, wildly accessible and even more mind-blowingly sexy. Did he have a turn-on switch for that smile? Was he even aware of how powerful it was?

She blushed, chin resting on her knees, her brown eyes unwavering.

'Okay!' Sergio flung his arms wide in a gesture that was a mixture of frustration and amused resignation. 'So I'm realistic in my approach to relationships? I never make promises I'm in danger of not keeping. I don't encourage slumber parties. At this stage in my life I'm not interested in playing for keeps…'

'And you're always on the lookout for anyone who wants to get too close just because you're rich…?'

'That's right.' His expression cooled.

'Because you've had a bad experience?' Susie mused.

'You could say that,' he drawled, relaxing. 'And now is the question-and-answer session over?'

Susie didn't answer. She was staring into space. He'd been hurt—badly hurt—by someone he'd trusted who had turned out to be after his money. She wondered what this mysterious woman looked like, had been like… It didn't matter in the big picture, because she wasn't going to get involved with him, but she was curious nevertheless.

Had he been madly in love with her?

Her stomach gave a little flip, because she couldn't imagine him being madly in love with anyone. Even after only her brief contact with him he struck her as a man in total control of every aspect of his life.

What woman had had the power to bring this big, powerful man to his knees? She must have been quite something. Hence his learning curve...

'Stop trying to work me out.'

'Huh?' Susie blinked and focused on him.

'You're trying to piece me together,' Sergio said wryly. 'Don't. We can enjoy one another without too much in-depth analysis. Come and sit closer to me. It's driving me crazy, seeing you and not being able to touch.'

Susie stood up, flexed her muscles, which had stiffened. and glanced at the roses taking up half her flat.

'You're going to have to take most of these back to your apartment,' she said, buying time—because there was still a stubborn part of her that didn't want to fall into his arms at the snap of his fingers. She felt like someone with one foot hanging off the edge of a cliff, even though she didn't know why because, as he'd said, mutual lust didn't involve the depth charge of a proper relationship...

This was going to be an adventure that would take her right out of her comfort zone.

She had tried the online dating in search of a soul mate and had found three losers and a would-be loser. She had been out with guys who had been the last word in fun, who had been laid-back and full of creative spark, and she had only been tempted to get close to one of them— and that one had ended up being just a little too much *fun* for her liking.

Sergio Burzi occupied a place of his own. He had laid his cards on the table. He wanted sex and nothing more. She wasn't even really sure what he thought of her. Did he still think that she was after what he could give her?

It sounded so weirdly *clinical*—even though sex was the least clinical thing on the face of the earth.

She didn't do clinical—not when it came to emotions—but...

What he aroused in her was so overwhelming. She just had to look at his cool, handsome face, just had to hear the deep timbre of his voice, and all her reservations flew out of her head.

She felt his eyes follow her as she strolled towards the window and then turned to look at him.

'When you do, I'll help you put them in vases. Or something...'

Sergio relaxed. He hadn't even known how much he wanted this. 'It'll have to be the *something*...my apartment lacks vases. It's the first time I will have had flowers returned to me...'

But there was a first time for everything.

Admittedly he had never factored that into his life before, but he was willing to go along for the ride...until, of course, the ride became boring and it was time to get off...

CHAPTER FOUR

BUT RIGHT NOW...

He shut out the nagging little things that didn't add up. Who cared? She wasn't being interviewed for the job of being his life partner. This was about lust. This was about sex. He knew from experience that the physical never lasted, however good it was. Sooner rather than later tedium began to set in, and no amount of intellectual sparring could stanch the tide once it had begun.

The advantage of going out with high-powered career women was that they had less potential to become clingy. They had jobs, careers...there wasn't any danger of them becoming dependent, needy, demanding.

He frowned, distracted by his train of thought.

'Penny for them?' Susie said lightly.

'Come again?'

'You're frowning.' She was drawn to sit right next to him, nestle into him, and she fought off the weakness. He would be very used to getting what he wanted from a woman. So even if this *was* all about physical attraction surely they could spend a little time talking.

'It happens occasionally.' Sergio focused on her with lazy intensity.

'*Why* are you frowning? You must have everything you could possibly want in life. Although...' she chewed her

lip thoughtfully '…it's not all about money and posses-
sions, is it? I mean, you have an apartment that most people
would kill for, but there's more to life than a fancy apartment and a fast car…'

'Are you about to launch into homilies about money not
being the be-all and end-all?'

'You're so cynical.'

'I prefer to call it realistic.' He patted the space next to
him and she shuffled along the sofa so that she was sitting
a bit closer, with her legs crossed.

Sergio suppressed a sigh of frustration. Why had he
thought that this might be a straightforward affair? Two
adults attracted to one another who could enjoy one other
in a fleeting, no-strings-attached situation? Had he really
been stupid enough to imagine that some flowers would
seamlessly pave the way?

'I've never been that convinced about the advantages
of being realistic,' Susie said pensively. 'I mean, I think
optimism is much more important.'

Sergio detected the sound of warning bells ringing.
'Which is precisely why I'm not your type,' he inserted
smoothly.

'I wish you would stop reminding me of that. It just
makes it hard for me to think about doing something that's
not going to last. I'm not an idiot. I know relationships
end all the time. But I never thought I'd be the kind of
person who gets involved with someone when I know it's
not going anywhere. I never thought I'd waste my time
like that.'

'That's because this is probably the first time in your
life that you've fallen prey to that little thing called desire.' He reached out and lazily stroked her wrist. 'The red
dress was more obvious, but this shapeless outfit of yours
is doing all sorts of interesting things to my system… Are

you wearing a bra? No, I don't think you are… Shuffle a bit closer and I can find out one way or the other. Of course if you *are* wearing a bra then it's going to have to come off, because I want to feel your breasts in my hands…'

Susie's breathing quickened. How was she supposed to think when he was saying stuff like that? And was he right? Was she feeling like this, behaving like this, because he turned her on as no one ever had in her life before?

'I…I…I've had a boyfriend,' she said weakly, clinging to the conversation even though talking was getting difficult when he was looking at her like that, his eyes all brooding and sexy and *intense*. 'I know what…physical attraction is all about…'

'Do you?' He held the bottom of her jumper between his fingers and gave a gentle tug, which was enough to make her eyelids flutter and her breathing hitch in her throat even more.

No! He was right—she didn't know a thing about desire…at least not desire like this, which was eating her up, devouring her, making her want to pass out from its intensity…

'I don't believe you. I can feel you throbbing for me. You're hot and you're wet and you don't know how much longer you can sit there with your legs crossed, pretending to hold a normal conversation.'

'You don't know *everything*.'

'When it comes to sex you'd be shocked at how much I know.'

'I'm not sure I want to hear that.'

'You want me to touch you… I know you want to hear that. And you can't *begin* to imagine how much I want to touch you. Why do you think I came here? This is one of those rare occasions when I've done something that makes very little sense…'

Susie liked the sound of that. She liked the thought that she might be driving him a little crazy. Because he was driving *her* more than a little crazy and she wanted him to touch her so badly that she could scarcely think straight.

'I'm not wearing a bra,' she muttered, excited and shocked by the brazenness of that admission.

'Let me see.'

Her hands were trembling as she lifted the jumper. *Was she really doing this?* Her breasts felt heavy, sensitive, her nipples pulsing. She had squeezed her eyes tightly shut but now she half opened them to sneak a glance at his face and the heat in his eyes made her giddy.

'You're beautiful,' Sergio muttered. He pressed his hand against his erection to try and control it.

Her breasts were big, her nipples huge pink discs. She projected the air of someone who was unfamiliar with stripping off...shy, hesitant.

Was that image correct? He didn't give a damn. He just knew that he wanted her.

With a stifled groan he pulled her and she toppled onto him, her breasts squashing against his chest, her heart racing.

They blindly found each other's lips and the probing of his tongue lit her up like a spark set to dry tinder. Her fingers curled into his hair and she squirmed against him, his clothes a horrible, unwanted barrier between them. When he drew back she hungrily reached forward, kissing the side of his mouth, his neck, breathing softly and erratically against his cheek.

'I'm too big for this sofa,' Sergio muttered unsteadily. 'Tell me you have a real bed here and not some fold-out nonsense.'

'I have a bed. It creaks.'

'That'll do.'

She didn't know how they made their way to the bedroom. She just knew that they did. She just knew that she found herself lying on her double bed, which took up most of the room, and watching as he slowly...very slowly... began removing his clothes.

She couldn't peel her eyes away. The constant pale light from the street lamps outside illuminated the room just sufficiently for her to appreciate the awesome, powerful masculinity of his body.

He was honed to physical perfection. Broad, bronzed shoulders and a broad chest with a dusky coating of hair tapered to a slim waist and lean hips. Sometime, while doing whatever he did to be able to afford his standard of living, he must surely get around to doing lots of gruelling exercise.

Her eyes dipped as he stepped out of his boxers, and widened at his impressive erection.

More than anything in the world she wanted to touch herself, to alleviate some of the desperate need coursing through her body.

She marvelled that he could see anything in her at all. Okay, so her intellect might leave him a bit cold, but surely someone that sinfully sexy couldn't be attracted to *her*?

But he was.

It was there in his eyes and in a certain stillness about him—as if he was doing his utmost to control himself.

'Like what you see?'

Some inarticulate choked sound managed to emerge and he grinned.

'I'm taking that as a *yes*...' He strolled towards the side of the bed, watching her watching him. 'Touch me,' he ordered huskily.

Susie propped herself up, touched him delicately, and drew courage from the way he reacted—his big erection stiffening even more and a half-heard hiss escaping his lips.

She circled his girth with her hand and then flicked her tongue along the throbbing shaft. His big hand tangled in her hair, controlling her exploring mouth and the flicks of her tongue as she tasted him.

He shuddered…breathed in…exhaled jerkily…finally tugged her away from him, easing the pressure of his fingers in her hair and only slowly regaining his breath.

He arched back, his eyes closed, nostrils flaring. His eyes flickered open and met hers.

Sergio could feel her gentle breath on his erection as she stared up at him. Her blonde hair tumbled over his hand and spilled in curly tangles over her slender shoulders. She still had the wretched jogging bottoms on, but her full breasts hung like ripe fruit, succulent and tantalising.

He had to keep very still, hold himself together, because control was slipping through his fingers faster than a knife through butter. He breathed deeply, drinking her in, then lowered himself onto the bed next to her.

She shuffled to allow him room and flipped over onto her side.

'You have an amazing body,' she breathed in frank honesty, and Sergio raised his eyebrows, amused, because women might come on to to him but rarely were they so openly admiring.

She traced her finger along his collarbone, shivering with excitement, and circled one brown nipple.

'You must go to the gym a lot,' she murmured.

'When I find the time.'

He spread his hand over her stomach and eased it under the track pants and under her panties until he felt the downy softness of her pubic hair.

He parted the soft folds of her vagina and slipped his

finger into the honeyed dampness between her legs, finding the little bud of her clitoris and rubbing it gently until she was moaning with pleasure.

'You need to take these things off...' he said roughly. 'I'm doing my best to take things slowly, but I can't guarantee that my efforts are going to last much longer...'

'I can't believe we're doing this...'

'Let's save the incredulity for later. I'm going crazy.'

Too damned crazy to keep his hand down there. He tugged the joggers down and she wriggled out of them, taking her underwear at the same time and kicking both to the ground, and then she lay flat on the bed, twisting as he straddled her.

He didn't give her time to touch his erect penis. He couldn't. She had already done devastating things to his self-control when she had sucked him.

Now it was his turn. The only way he could try and get his self-control back where it belonged.

He rose up and gazed down at her as she lay there, spread naked beneath him. Her arms were stretched out and the bed was so stupidly small that the tips of her fingers practically touched either side of it. The mattress was lumpy and she was right. The bed creaked. It was anything but a four-poster creation, with satin sheets and gauze curtains, but he couldn't have been more turned on.

He would take his time.

Difficult when the scent of her filling his nostrils was like a drug.

He lowered his head, took one succulent nipple into his mouth and suckled on it, pulling it in and drawing deep, holding her firm as she wriggled like a little eel, hardly able to contain her mounting excitement.

Her hands kneaded his shoulders and she arched back, breathing fast, her nipple thrust into his mouth, her legs spread wide under him. He nudged between them with his knee, felt her wetness, and had to stop immediately or risk tipping over the edge.

Which would be a first—and not a first he wanted.

He steadied himself, switched to her other nipple, teasing it with his teeth and his tongue while he played with the other one, rubbing it between his fingers, gentle strokes that had her panting.

Her breasts were generous—more than generous, given her stature—but her stomach was flat, her waist slender.

He trailed a path down her ribcage, tickling her with his tongue, pausing only to circle her belly button, and she gave an embarrassed little yelp as he settled between her legs.

This was *not* the woman in the red dress. The woman in the red dress would have been a hell of a lot more experienced. The woman in the red dress would have played games, would have done her utmost to hold his interest by being inventive and acrobatic. No, this was the girl in the baggy jogging bottoms and the baggy sweatshirt, with no make-up and freckles scattered across the bridge of her nose.

And who *was* she?

He swept past that question, which had popped into his head from nowhere, because this was definitely not the time to be reflecting on who she was or what her motives were.

She was slick against his tongue, which he flicked into her and along the sensitive crease that sheathed her clitoris. He felt that little stiff bud and tickled it so that she groaned and arched her hips up, allowing him to cup her bottom with his hands.

Dazed, Susie looked down at the dark head moving between her thighs. Nothing in her life had prepared her for this level of eroticism. Part of her really couldn't believe she was allowing herself to drop all her inhibitions like this, and another part was relishing every single second of the experience.

She bucked against his mouth as she felt herself getting closer and closer to a climax and with a fierce groan he rose up and thrust into her—just one long, deep thrust, as though he couldn't stop himself. Just as quickly he withdrew with a muttered oath.

'What's wrong…? You can't stop now… Please…'

'I need to get a condom. I can't *believe*…'

He couldn't believe that he had done the unthinkable—that he had been so turned on that he had entered her without protection, even for a split second.

He placed the condom on with fingers that weren't quite steady, and this time…

One deep thrust.

He was huge, thick and hard inside her, and it felt so good that she wanted to scream out loud. He began moving, easing himself deeper inside her, moving faster.

Susie wrapped her arms around his neck, her breasts bouncing as their movements meshed until they were moving as one, totally in sync.

Her orgasm was overpowering—shooting her into orbit and subsiding so gradually that it seemed to last for ever—and then she knew that he had come as well, felt his whole body stiffen and heard him groan out loud.

He rolled off her and shielded his face with his arm.

This was normally the moment when his mind began slowly but inexorably turning to work. It was amazing how easily he found it to focus on problems and ongoing deals in the aftermath of lovemaking.

Most times he would allow his body a few minutes to subside, then he would be on his feet, heading for the shower, eyeing the laptop which was always within handy reach.

Tonight was different. She nestled against him, and his instinctive urge to ease her away from that sort of compromising position was absent.

Which was odd, considering he had so many reservations about her.

'Was I okay?' she asked shyly, splaying her fingers on his chest and ruffling the dark hair which was so masculine and sexy.

Sergio didn't think anyone had ended a hot lovemaking session with him with that question on her lips, and he smiled and stroked the hair away from her flushed face.

'Terrible,' he said gravely, and then grinned when she tapped him lightly on the arm after a moment's horrified hesitation. 'Sorry—I meant brilliant,' he murmured, meaning every word of it.

'I didn't expect you to come here, you know...' Susie told him softly.

She lay back and stared up at the ceiling, which was in dire need of several coats of paint. She twisted so that she was looking at his profile.

Sergio sighed. Certain things had to be put straight, which was a nuisance—but, whatever and whoever she was, she needed to know that this was just something passing. A virus that would clear from his system in no time at all. He could feel her big brown eyes gazing at him, could feel the softness of her breasts against his arm, and he was startled when his body leapt into arousal once again.

'Sometimes the unexpected happens...' He addressed the ceiling, putting one hand on his erection and holding it firmly, because right now it wasn't going anywhere—not until he had said what he had to say.

He turned to her and breathed in her clean floral scent.

In actual fact this was a speech he never actually had to give—not in so many words. It was always understood that, whilst he might thoroughly enjoy a woman's company, it would be a mistake for her to start building castles in the sky. The women he dated generally got the unspoken message.

'Which,' he continued carefully, 'isn't to say that it necessarily means anything.'

'What do you mean?'

'I mean…put it this way…you told me that you favoured optimism over realism…'

'I said I favoured optimism over *cynicism*. What's the point in being cynical? How can you ever look forward to what life has to bring if you're busy seeing everything from a gloomy angle?'

Sergio was temporarily distracted. He thought, in passing, that she had amazing eyes—a curious shade of brown, milk chocolate in colour, and fringed with lush, dark lashes… And the tiny mole on her cheekbone was pretty cute as well.

'It's extraordinary that you can face each day brimming over with optimism when you live *here*…'

'That an incredibly snobby thing to say.'

'You're probably right.' He flushed darkly. Stanley had said more or less the same thing to him, earlier in the evening.

'You can come from money and still empathise with people who haven't got any…'

'Of *course* I empathise with people who don't have money… Not that it's particularly relevant, but Stanley, my driver, doesn't come from an exalted background!' He raked his fingers through his hair and wondered how they had ended up down this blind alley.

'That's not *empathising*—that's *recognising*…there's

a difference. Although…' she relented and met his eyes squarely '…it's pretty cool what you did for him.'

'I beg your pardon?'

'He told me. About you helping him get back on his feet after he'd spent time in prison. He said that he pretty much wouldn't have known what to do if you hadn't stepped in and rescued him from himself.'

'Stanley *told* you that…? He *never* talks about his past. For God's sake—he was supposed to deliver you back to your apartment, not launch into an explanation of his life experiences. I'll have to have a word with him. Discretion is always—but *always*—the better part of valour when it comes to the business of being a chauffeur.'

'Please don't! People confide in me… I'll be mortified if you go to him and tell him off for opening up…'

Sergio could scarcely believe that his driver *had* 'opened up'. He wasn't the *opening up* kind. 'People confide in you…?'

'It's one of the things I do really well. I make people feel comfortable…' She laughed self-consciously. 'It's one of my few talents.'

'How did we get on to this?'

'I don't know. You were telling me… Well, actually, you were telling me that the fact you showed up here doesn't mean anything.'

She couldn't bear the thought of hearing him inform her in that dark, bone-melting voice of his that he'd had his fill and it was time to say goodbye. Maybe he would tell her that she was worth every rose he had sunk his money into.

Had he said anything when she had jokingly told him that she'd help stick them in vases at his apartment because he would have to take most of them away? She couldn't remember. Her brain felt fuzzy, caught up with trying to predict what he was going to say.

'I know it doesn't,' she said lightly, because it seemed a better idea to take the bull by the horns than to wait for it to destroy the shop.

'It doesn't. I'm not interested in forging a relationship with you, Susie.'

'I know. I'm not your type,' she interjected quickly, before he could really get going on something truly hurtful.

'Even if you were...'

'You mean, even if I was one of those high-powered, my-career-is-everything types?'

'If you want to put it that way... Even if you were one of those, I still wouldn't be interested in any kind of relationship.'

'Why is that? Don't you ever want to settle down?'

'I expect I will one day,' Sergio said with a shrug, 'and when I do I'll make sure I choose a woman with whom it seems a workable proposition. I'm not on the hunt for emotional ties.'

He had bitter first-hand knowledge of where emotional ties could lead. He had seen his father reduced by a girl who had played on his emotions and then used his weakness to take what she could. He had seen what happened when control was lost.

'Oh. I see.'

'Do you?'

'Yes.'

Suddenly lying naked next to him on the bed felt too intimate... She swung her legs over the side, avoiding hitting the wall with the soles of her feet from habit, and yanked at the blanket which she kept on her bed for those really cold nights when the tepid central heating just wasn't quite enough to warm her up, even when she was under her duvet.

She wrapped it around her and banged on the overhead

light in the process as she headed out of the door and to the little bathroom off to the side.

She needed to get her thoughts in order.

Sergio, on the verge of following her—because why the hell did she have to overreact to a perfectly simple word of warning?—stopped in his tracks and took notice of what had not been visible when they had stumbled into the bedroom.

The bookshelf at the side of the bed.

The top shelf groaned under the weight of art books and the remaining three shelves were crammed with illustrations of varying sizes painted onto hardboard, some of them overlapping. He went closer. They were exquisite. Very detailed. Some depicted birds or flowers, others recognisable cartoon characters in comic poses.

She hadn't been lying. Not about this, at any rate.

Of course it made no difference, he decided. She might not be the gold-digger he had first thought, but...

She was in the shower. He could hear it going and he roamed through her tiny sitting area, taking in all the expensive little trinkets that were dotted here and there.

So she had expensive tastes? Maybe she saved whatever little money she earned and splashed out on expensive stuff?

Or maybe they were presents from rich ex-lovers?

Not caring for the thought of that, he headed straight for the bathroom and pushed open the door. He hadn't expected it to have the sophistication of something as simple as a lock and he had been right. No lock.

She gave a startled shriek as he yanked back the shower curtain and he smiled drily when she tried to cover all her private parts with her hands—which left a cute little nipple showing, as well as some deliciously damp pubic hair peeping past her fingers.

'If you *don't mind*,' Susie nearly shouted, still seething because she had managed to ignore every single warning sign and fly into bed with someone who had filled her flat with stupid roses and was now trying to think of a way of dispatching her.

'I don't if you don't…' Sergio grinned slowly and then stepped into the shower with her.

He was far too tall, and far too broad, and it was beyond cramped but he didn't mind. Whether it was because he'd discovered those paintings, worked out that she had at least told the truth about one thing, whether she'd listened to his warnings or not, he knew that there was no doubt in his mind that this was just too damned good to end just yet…

'What are you doing? I don't want you in here with me!'

'Why not? I can reach lots of places you can't reach with the soap…' He cupped her protesting face in his hands and kissed her while the water streamed over them.

Susie tried her best to resist. She was confused. Could she do this? Was this really *her?* Was she a woman who could have a full-blown affair with a guy when she knew— *when she had been told in no uncertain terms*—that it was going nowhere?

Did a relationship have to go anywhere, anyway? Of course she was essentially a romantic, someone who believed in love and happy endings, but that wasn't life most of the time—and what was the point in denying herself the joy of adventure, the fun of searching, the excitement of the unknown in the meanwhile?

The forthcoming wedding and her anxious desire to show up with someone halfway decent had thrown everything out of proportion. She had suddenly become desperate to find someone suitable, to prove herself in her family's eyes…and desperation had made her lose perspective.

She didn't *need* guarantees of anything to have fun. He had been brutally honest and she had learnt a valuable lesson from that honesty: take what was on offer and ask for nothing more or else walk away right now...

'I was tactless,' Sergio murmured, drawing back and staring down at her. 'Forgive me.'

He reached for the bar of soap, rubbed at it until it lathered and then began to soap her, his body pressing against hers as though they were doing a very slow dance together. He soaped her back, her buttocks and then her stomach.

By the time his hands made it to her breasts she was no longer thinking straight. In fact she wasn't thinking at all.

'I'd suck your nipples,' he murmured, 'but this cramped space won't allow that sort of luxury. Next time we do anything under running water it's not going to be here. You'll have to settle for me playing with them instead... Like it? How much...? You have fantastic nipples...nice and big and very, *very* suckable... Shall I tell you what I'd *really* like to do now?'

'No! You're turning me on too much...'

'I like that. We could head for the bed, but I'm enjoying this experience...enjoying thinking about how much more we could do if we had just a little more space... I could get down on my knees and taste you down there... would you like that?'

'Stop...' she begged.

She wanted him inside her so badly that it hurt, but he was right. The shower cubicle was fashioned on the same small scale as everything else in the flat. She couldn't even let him lift her onto him—couldn't wrap her legs around his body, couldn't let him penetrate her that way. Not without paramedics getting involved.

'Play with me,' he urged. 'There are other ways of getting some satisfaction...'

He moved under the water, his hand pressed against the tiled wall, his powerful body jerking as she excited him with her hand until he had descended from his climax.

Her body was craving fulfilment. She parted her legs and moaned softly as he slipped his fingers into her. With his hand on her back, he manoeuvred her until he found the perfect position, the perfect place to bring her to her own shuddering orgasm.

She flung back her head, not caring that he was looking at her in her most intensely private moment, and her whole body stiffened as those magical fingers stroked and rubbed, fast then slow, hard then gentle, taking her to the very peak of physical pleasure.

The water was beginning to go cold when she was once again breathing evenly, her eyes drowsy with satisfaction.

Sergio switched off the shower and then dried her off, very tenderly.

She was spent. She felt like a rag doll, quite happy for him to take her in hand.

'I'm sorry if I've offended you by being blunt,' he said, once he'd sat her down in the sitting room, with her bathrobe around her and a cup of coffee in her hand. 'I just wanted to make sure that there weren't any mixed messages.'

'I know.' Susie sipped her coffee and realised this was what it was—his way of gently but firmly reminding her of the conditions for whatever relationship they enjoyed. It wasn't going to last. He was giving her an out.

The dozens and dozens of roses were proof of how much he wanted her…but if she didn't agree to his terms and conditions there would be no more of those. The pursuit would be well and truly over.

'I'm not a kid, whatever you might believe. I'm not after your money either. I can look after myself, and I understand perfectly what you're saying to me. No involvement except of a sexual kind.' She shrugged. 'A little light-hearted fun…sounds like a brilliant idea…'

Sergio dealt her a slashing smile. 'Good.' Midnight-blue eyes fixed on her with immense satisfaction. 'Come lie on me, in that case, and tell me all about those paintings I saw in your bedroom…'

CHAPTER FIVE

THE WRETCHED WEDDING was here. In the thrill of being with Sergio she had forgotten about it, even though her mother and her sister had made sure to remind her at frequent intervals, had quizzed her as to whether she had bought a dress.

Susie wondered whether they expected her to show up in an artist's smock with a paintbrush stuck behind her ear. Or maybe wearing a pair of jeans and a tee shirt and trainers, because she always left the 'looking smart' stuff to Alex, who did it so much better. Alex was tall, leggy, brunette, sophisticated. Clothes just always seemed to hang better on her.

Being five foot four, prone to looking round, with wild blonde hair that strenuously resisted the call of straighteners was always going to be a challenge to smart outfits.

But she *had* bought a dress and now, sitting cross-legged on her bed, she stared at it without really seeing it at all.

Of course Sergio wouldn't be going with her. Even though they had now been seeing one another for nearly two months—two blissful, sexy, passionate months.

She felt a lump in her throat and tears begin to gather at the back of her eyes, because soon it was all going to have to draw to a painful close. Painful for her, at any rate.

She had only gone and disobeyed his orders not to get

involved, not to see what they had as anything more than what it was—fantastic sex. It was the lynchpin of their relationship. They couldn't keep their hands off one another. He had confessed that he was surprised, because he had expected it to fizzle out after a couple of weeks, and she had taken that to mean that however good the sex was she really didn't have what it took to hold his interest.

Not the way he held hers. The way that made her want more…the way that made her think of commitment and permanence…the way that made her crave a future and plans that went further than what they were going to do the following evening.

She wouldn't be seeing him tonight because he was in New York, clinching a big deal. He had been gone two days and he would be gone two more, conveniently over the wedding weekend, so she hadn't even had to skirt round the issue.

Not that he would have volunteered to come anyway. She had grudgingly confessed that the reason she had been so idiotically tempted into online dating had been to see whether the love of her life might have materialised out there, so that she could show him off at her cousin's wedding and kill all those muted whispers about when she was going to find herself a decent guy.

He had grinned and told her that he had never heard such a crazy reason for dating losers who went online to see what they could catch.

She lay down on the bed and stared up at the ceiling, considering her options.

Next to her was the little stick with the bright blue lines announcing that her life as she knew it was over.

Pregnant!

He had been beyond careful every single time they had made love except for that very first time, when he had moved inside her and then withdrawn almost immediately—but not fast enough, because he had left behind enough of himself to create the little tiny life that was beating away inside her now.

He was going to go mad.

He was going to run faster than a speeding bullet.

Oh, yes, he would do the decent thing by her financially, but he didn't do long-term relationships.

She was facing a sea change and there would be no one by her side. Her parents were going to be disappointed. Her mother would shake her head and try to find a silver lining somewhere. Her father would make noises about her moving back home to live with them—although they spent most of their time out of the country anyway, so it wasn't as though they would be around for babysitting duties. She and Alex had had nannies from birth, so it was unlikely that a surprise grandchild would suddenly convert her parents into the sort of people who would enjoy pushing a pram in the park and feeding the ducks.

And Alex would be disappointed as well. *How could you have been so careless? Contraception is free, Susie! So that this sort of thing can be prevented!* She could almost hear her sister's voice ringing in her ears.

Disappointment all round.

A wave of self-pity washed over her. Just when she was beginning to build up a steady base with her freelance work, just when she was on the verge of getting a commission from one of the museums to illustrate the natural history section for a book to be brought out the following year...

Her cell phone buzzed and she glanced at Sergio's number and debated whether she should just let it ring. He had called her at least twice a day since he had been in New York.

'Hi.'

She couldn't resist hearing the deep drawl of his sexy voice. Even from across the Atlantic it still managed to do weird and wonderful things to her tummy.

But she knew that she sounded flat, and she decided that she didn't care because soon there would be no more of him anyway.

She wasn't quite sure when she would break the news. No rush. She had to take time out to get her head round it herself before she started trying to cope with his horror.

'What's wrong?'

'Nothing.' She tried to inject her usual ready laugh into her voice, but it petered out into a sigh and she lacked the energy to take it up a notch.

Instead, she asked him what he was doing, how his deal was going, whether he had sorted it out. They never talked about his work. She knew he did high-powered stuff involving complicated finance and tricky acquisitions. And she now had a better idea of just how much he owned. Enormous amounts of money. Companies all over the place—from restaurants to a publishing house.

However, she just didn't have it in her to get detailed when it came to showing her interest—which, she guessed, was just one of those chasms between them. His future would include a woman who understood the ins and outs of what he did and could fully follow if he chose to discuss the details.

Thinking about that brought her right back to a future he certainly wouldn't want—and that would be one with a child he hadn't banked on and a woman he fundamentally didn't see as having a lasting place in his life.

'Huh?' She surfaced to realise that he had asked her something.

'Spit it out, Susie. What's bugging you? You've just

asked me about my deal, which is something you never do, and you haven't said a word about what you've been doing. Where's my sexy chatterbox disappeared to?'

Susie stiffened. Sexy. Chatterbox. *That* was what she represented to him, she thought with unusual bitterness. She was someone to get into bed with who talked a lot. She bored him with inane chatter about her work, her illustrations, conversations she'd had with random people during the course of the day, gossip she'd shared with her friends, all their escapades and little adventures. He always listened, but that wasn't to say that he listened *with interest*, was it? He listened because it came as part of the package deal that included the sex he was always reminding her was the best he'd ever had.

'You're not angsting over that wedding, are you?' Sergio drawled drily.

Should he tell her that he had decided to surprise her there with his presence? He really didn't want her getting the wrong idea, and weddings were occasions when wrong ideas could easily start taking shape, but he wanted to fill in some missing pieces. He wasn't into meeting the family members of the women he slept with, but for someone so open she was reticent when it came to family stories.

What was she hiding? He might not be in it for the long haul but he didn't like secrets. Secrets made him uneasy. He liked knowing the layout of the land around him. He liked control, and if that meant meeting her relatives, then so be it. He wanted a complete picture. The picture might throw up all the suspicions he had had of her in the beginning again, and then it would be a shame but he would have to get rid of her.

And, on a more fundamental level, he was missing the feel of her responsive little body.

'Er...yes, I guess so...' Susie clung to this lifeline.

'You know...there'll be so many people there...relatives I haven't seen for a million years...all that small talk...'

'You're good at small talk.' He shook off the uncomfortable thought that he wanted to believe what she told him.

She gritted her teeth. 'And I'm beginning to think that I should have got the blue dress instead of this brown one. Brown's such a drab colour.'

So he thought she was only good for sex and small talk? Well, she might just as well live down to his expectations! She droned about the dress with suitable enthusiasm until she began boring herself.

'You looked sexy as hell when you tried it on for me...' Sergio murmured, thinking ahead to ripping it off her. Or maybe he wouldn't. Maybe he would just push the flimsy fabric up and take her while she was still dressed to kill. Maybe he would insist that she left on the high stilettos...

He relaxed, comfortable with thoughts of the fantastic sex they would have. A quiet place somewhere...assuming there would *be* a quiet place...because he had no idea where the venue was.

He only knew that the wedding was being held in the country somewhere. Berkshire. Probably a town hall...or a village pub... He had the address, but it meant nothing to him because he rarely saw fit to venture outside London.

'In fact...' He dropped his voice a couple of levels, 'I've been having some rather interesting fantasies involving that dress...'

Susie didn't want to hear. She didn't want to be reminded that she was just all about the sex and the small talk. She also didn't want to feel the liquid she was now feeling pooling between her legs, making her want to touch herself right here, right now.

'Shouldn't you be focusing on your work...and...er... not having...fantasies about me in a drab brown dress...?'

'You're cute when you fish for compliments, Susie...'

'I was doing no such thing!'

'Of course you were. You want me to tell you that the dress isn't brown...and it isn't drab—at least not on you. You want me to tell you that those chiffon layers give just enough of a hint of what's underneath to drive any sane man crazy with desire... You want me to tell you that if you were wearing that dress for me and me alone I'd insist you don't wear a bra. But, considering you won't be, then you're under orders to wear your sturdiest, least attractive bra—because I don't want any other man's eyes lingering too long on your breasts...those breasts are for my eyes only...'

'Stop...' She hated the way he could make her blood run hot in her veins, the way he could make her blush and giggle and could drive every coherent thought from her head.

'I wouldn't stop,' he murmured huskily, glancing down at his watch and realising that in under fifteen minutes someone would tap him on the shoulder and tell him that he was ready to board, 'but I've got to run. And...'

'Time is money. Yes. I know.' It was what he always said, in that teasing voice of his, and it had become their private mantra—which was just one of the stupid little things that had lulled her into falling in love with him. One of the shared jokes which made their relationship feel so intimate to her but which really didn't mean anything to him at all.

She remembered the pregnancy test stick, temporarily forgotten, which was on the bed next to her.

'I'm not sure I can see you on Sunday evening when you get back,' she said flatly. 'Things aren't going to end until quite late Saturday night...probably not until the early hours of Sunday morning...and I'm thinking I might just hang around for the rest of Sunday there...catch up with all those relatives I haven't seen in such a long time...'

'I thought catching up with the relatives you haven't seen in a long time was one of the things bugging you about going in the first place…?'

'There are quite a few I do actually want to see…so… Maybe next week we can…er…meet up…?'

Normally she would be hopping up and down at the thought of seeing him, not politely putting him off, but these weren't normal times, were they? Normal times were at an end, and she had to start laying the foundations for her eventual withdrawal. She had to train herself to get used to not having him around—and widening the gaps between the times when they saw one another was step one on that road.

Her mind fogged over. Because there were now so many steps on this new road that she wasn't sure where to put the first one.

'No problem,' Sergio said easily, thinking that she would be seeing him a whole lot sooner than she anticipated.

'No problem?'

'I'll call you.'

'Right. Yes. Call me.'

'Really have to go now… I'll see you when I see you…'

He disconnected. Susie stared at her mobile phone, heart thudding. He hadn't expressed any disappointment at the thought that he wouldn't be seeing her the weekend when he returned from New York.

Was he tiring of her? Had she reached her sell-by date? She had always known that it existed, but now that it was staring her in the face she felt sick, desperate with longing, panicked at the thought that he might be in the process of dumping her, and angry with herself for not being stronger when it was going to happen anyway—just as soon as she detonated her bomb under his carefully organised life.

She barely slept at all, woke the following morning far later than she had planned, and then spent the remainder of the morning rushing around, trying to do clever things with her hair, looking at the clock, and frantically wrapping the present she had bought in paper she had designed herself but unfortunately not in quite the right size, so that she had to camouflage the gap with ordinary brown paper and very wide ribbon.

In between all of this she kept stopping in front of the mirror, gazing at her still flat stomach and wondering what was going on inside.

The wedding ceremony kicked off at three, at the small church in the village where her aunt and uncle lived. It was the sort of picture-postcard-perfect place that only the super-rich could afford. No one would ever guess that it was a thriving commuter hub for many of those top businessmen who had to get into the City, where they could earn sufficient money to install their families in the rolling mansions and quaint cottages that dotted that part of Berkshire.

As a child, she and Alex had always enjoyed making the trip down to see Clarissa. Their own parents, Louise and Robert Sadler, had lived further north, and being close to London had seemed like a grand adventure whenever they had ventured south.

Clarissa and her husband-to-be, Thomas, at twenty-two and twenty-eight respectively, were good candidates for the Berkshire lifestyle. He was an up-and-coming barrister and she was destined to be the perfect stay-at-home wife.

On the way out of her flat Susie paused to look at her reflection in the mirror again and thought to herself that Clarissa might have beaten both she and Alex up the aisle, much to her mother's dismay, but *she* would be the first to deliver a grandchild.

Even if, she thought with a grimace, the standing ovation might be a little muted.

She had planned on taking the train and then a taxi to the church, but on the spur of the moment she threw parsimony to the winds and decided on a taxi for the entire trip.

It meant dipping into the trust fund which she had always refused to touch, because it was there for when she decided to find somewhere to buy, but she honestly couldn't face the hassle of the train station in her wedding outfit.

Not when her thoughts were all over the place. Not when she felt sick with tension at the unexpected future in front of her. Definitely not when she thought of Sergio and the way he had casually dismissed her.

Outside, it was the perfect day for an early spring wedding. The skies were blue and cloudless, and the air was crisp rather than cold. Coats were needed, but thin ones, and there was no mud anywhere for delicate high heels to subside into.

Clarissa would be thrilled to bits. She had always had an uncanny ability to make people and things in general fall in line with what she wanted, and lo and behold the weather was being obedient.

Susie grinned, relaxing as she was driven to the church and only tensing once more when she was deposited outside, to join the two-hundred-strong throng of people piled in front.

Immediately her parents descended, followed by her sister, and for the next two hours there was blessed reprieve from her thoughts.

With all the romance in her soul she was tearful during the ceremony, and proud as punch at the stunning picture her cousin made in her meringue of a wedding dress, befitting a girl who had spent the first eight years of her life believing that she was a fairy princess.

There were hundreds of photos outside the church, and then the bride and groom left for Clarissa's parents' house in a white Bentley. Everyone else made their way the five miles or so in assorted cars.

Susie, sandwiched between her mother and her sister, half listened to Alex telling them about her new promotion, which would see her in line to become the youngest ever neurosurgeon at one of the leading hospitals in London. When there was eventually a lull in the conversation she half-heartedly told them that she was finally beginning to see some light in trying to track down clients for her illustrations.

At least her mother had steered clear of talking about guys so far.

'Susannah, darling, what's happening on the man front with you? I thought you might have surprised us by bringing a nice young man with you to the wedding...'

'Er...they're thin on the ground, Mother...all getting snapped up by beauty queens like Clarissa...'

'Darling, you look perfectly charming today...'

'What about all the other days?' Susie asked wryly.

Louise Sadler gave her a fond pat on the arm. 'You could add to your wardrobe of jeans with some more feminine clothes...you look an absolute dream in dresses...'

'A *bad* dream.'

Up ahead, the mansion that was Kate and Richard Princeton's house rose splendidly into view.

'The house looks nice. I like the lanterns lining the sides of the drive...'

'It's all a bit much, if you ask me, but you know my sister...she's never been able to resist the lure of trying to impress everyone... Still, I suppose Clarissa *is* the first in the Thornton line to get married. Hopefully you'll be next...'

'Or Alex.' She poked her sister in the ribs and Alex

instantly chipped in that there was no time even to *think* about marriage—not when she was building a demanding career that ate up most of her leisure time.

Alex was just the sort of woman Sergio was drawn to. She, Susie, was the exception that proved the rule. Wasn't that why she had never mentioned her high-achieving family? Because she didn't want any comparisons? Because she wanted to keep living in a little bubble where she was appreciated in her own right? If he never met her family then he would never take a step back and wonder what the heck he was doing with *her*.

It was a mortifying thought, tapping into her own silly insecurities, and she fought against it, knowing that it wasn't fair.

In the bigger scheme of things, silly insecurities were the least of her problems.

'I myself am not a believer in marriage,' she declared, to the astonishment of both her mother and her sister, and also her father, who craned back and looked at her with raised bushy eyebrows.

'Since when?' he demanded.

'Since…er…living in London…' she said airily. 'I guess I finally see that it's perfect for an independent woman to live her life without a guy in the background, nagging about when the dinner's going to be put on the table while he watches the footie…'

'You really *do* need to get rid of those young men you seem to like hanging around with…' Louise Sadler gave a little moue of distaste.

'And just for the record…' this as her father's driver was pulling into the courtyard, making a graceful turn before pulling to a stop and rushing round to open doors '…I think in this day and age it's absolutely acceptable for a woman to bring a child up on her own! You could say I'm a changed person—forging ahead…pretty much a feminist… It took me a while to get there, but better late than never!'

She leapt out of the car and immediately immersed herself in the nearest group of guests hovering by the front door. But she was nervously perspiring, relieved that neither of her parents had had the chance to follow up on that remark.

No drinking. Just one measly glass of champagne. She wondered how on earth she would make it stretch until one in the morning.

She knew a huge amount of the invited guests. There were relatives from all corners of the globe. But she'd barely had a chance to chat to the bride and groom—just a few snatched words of congratulation.

The marquee, which dominated much of the enormous back garden, was a thing of splendour, with lots of white swirling drapes and chandeliers. The flower arrangements on the tables were so huge that they would struggle to get through her front door, and they would take up more space in her sitting room than…

Than a hundred assorted roses.

She and Sergio had transported most of them back to his place the morning after he had brought them for her, had laughed and then fallen into bed—and had kept falling into bed because they couldn't *not*.

She felt a lump in her throat, and was on the verge of pinning a bright smile on her face to cover the moment of sadness when a voice behind her drawled, 'Don't burst into tears. It'll look like sour grapes…'

Susie swung round, shocked to her very core, scarcely believing her eyes.

She'd been standing at the very edge of the garden, half concealed by dense shrubbery, nursing her single glass of champagne. He had crept up on her, unobserved, and for a few breathless seconds she was lost for words.

'Surprised?' Sergio asked softly.

If she was, then she couldn't be more surprised than *he* was. He had had no reason to question his assumption that she came from humble origins. So she had a couple of expensive things in her flat...? Certainly not enough to make him think that she was anything but a girl venturing out in a fairly hazardous profession. He had assumed that whilst she might have *moral* support from her family, that was pretty much it on the support front.

In fact he had dared to question Stanley's map-reading skills, only realising that he was, indeed, at the right place when the car drove up the lantern-lined drive.

And now here he was.

And there *she* was. Staring at him as though she expected him to disappear in a puff of smoke.

'What are you doing here?' Susie demanded.

He looked perfect. Every inch the drop-dead gorgeous, brooding alpha male who had stolen her heart.

'I couldn't resist the prospect of pulling you behind the bushes and having my wicked way. Something about that dress...'

'You're supposed to be wrapping up a deal in New York.'

'I like breaking with the expected now and again. Where's the radiant bride and the lucky groom? I have to say...this isn't what I was anticipating...'

Susie flushed guiltily. She knew why she hadn't breathed a word about her family—knew that if she had he would have seen her as just another little rich kid, all caught up in doing nothing much because she knew that she could be bailed out of her discomfort if she got bored or fed up. Why would someone like him want to go out with someone like that?

'What *did* you anticipate?'

'Why did you let me assume that you were penniless?'

'I didn't let you assume anything. Did you decide to come here so that you could check out my background?'

'Comes with the terrain,' he answered coolly. 'We've been lovers for over two months. I like to know exactly what I'm getting into.'

'And what if you'd found that you'd "got into" someone from a council house background? Or worse…a criminal background…? Would you have got out of it pronto?'

'I don't deal in hypothetical situations. At any rate, I never took you for someone from a long line of train robbers…'

That said it all, she thought.

Suddenly everything seemed very complicated. Her parents would adore him. He was just the kind of guy they'd been hoping she would bring home one day. But what was the point of introducing them to someone who wasn't going to be around for very long? And when she broke the news to them that she was pregnant…

Susie blanched. They would immediately know the identity of the father. Did she want that? Would her parents make it their duty to confront him? They were very traditional.

She felt that she hadn't thought anything through—but then how could she? She'd barely had time to digest the revelation herself.

'You shouldn't have come,' she told him flatly.

Sergio looked at her through narrowed eyes. 'Not the response I was expecting…'

'This isn't a normal relationship, Sergio. This is…*sex*—and meeting my family isn't part of the deal…' She had to say it because she needed to start distancing herself.

'But I'm here now…'

'Not because you wanted to come as my partner.' She looked up at him steadily. 'In a normal relationship we would have travelled here together. You would have *wanted* to meet my parents, wanted to take that next step into the future…a future of getting to know one another's family and friends…'

'Where has *this* come from?'

'Does it matter? I'm just telling it like it is. You showed up here to do a background check on me… I suppose now that you're here and my family has passed muster it's all right for you to meet them?'

'You've managed to blow all this out of proportion and I'm wondering why…'

Dark eyes that saw far too much rested on her flushed face and Susie did her best to get her breathing under control.

'I'm a little stressed,' she muttered, looking down. 'It's not every day the guy you're going out with decides to check up on your family to make sure they're not escaped convicts.'

'That's not the only reason I came.'

Sergio was willing to let this go. What they had was good—better than good. He didn't want her to start getting ideas about his place in her life because she was at her cousin's wedding. He didn't need long, intense conversations about normal relationships, where boyfriends couldn't wait to meet the family and have friends over for Sunday lunch.

'Isn't it? What, then?'

'I missed you.' He smiled slowly.

'Why is it all about sex for you?'

She could read that smile as easily as she could read a book, and it still had the power to turn her legs to jelly even though her mind was doing its best to resist.

'It's not. Making money ranks highly as well. Ah. I spot curious eyes and a few people descending... Looks like you're going to have to do a round of introductions whether you like it or not.'

So he'd wanted to show up unannounced...? He couldn't see what the big deal was. When he had started this fling with her he had not expected it to last longer than a week or two. She didn't fit his profile, and he was smart enough to work out that if the women who *did* fit his profile were done and dusted within a month or two then there was no chance that her novelty value would outlast a night in the sack, maybe two.

But she was still around, and he wasn't sick of her yet... And, that being the case, it had made sense to see her in her own surroundings—the surroundings she had always made sure to keep quiet about. He had wanted to know exactly what he was dealing with instead of taking her at face value. That was just the man he was. Where was the problem?

She was still looking at him with wounded, accusing, angry eyes.

'You know where I'm coming from,' he said flatly. 'I don't need you getting weepy and hysterical. I came here to make sure you weren't playing some kind of long game. But, like I said, that wasn't the only reason. And now that I'm here there will be questions asked if you're sour and defiant about introducing your boyfriend to your family. So relax, Susie.'

She'd forgotten just how inherently suspicious he was, but it had been brought back to her now. She had fallen in love with a man who would only ever let her get so far and no further. There would always be part of him that was locked away. He was a charming, seductive lover, but a *proper* relationship would always threaten his self-control so he would never allow it. She'd conveniently managed to forget *that* part of him, and it hurt now to have been reminded of it.

'I'm relaxed!'

'You could have fooled me,' Sergio murmured. 'I think I know how to relax you, though...'

He kissed her on her mouth, felt a whisper of protest, and then she melted into him until he drew back and looked down at her with a sexy smile.

'Much better.'

'Mum! Alex...'

It *wasn't* much better. She might have been able to hide away in their private little bubble before, but now she had to stand up and be counted—because there was a third party on the scene: a baby. She couldn't keep going weak at the knees every time he glanced in her direction, pretending that the future was something that would take care of itself in due course.

'This is... This is...'

'I know who *you* are...'

Alex had moved into charming mode, and Susie sighed as she watched her older sister do what most women did when those deep, dark eyes fastened on them. Her brilliant, sharp, independent and undeniably striking sister *blushed*.

'Mother, this is only *Sergio Burzi*. I might be a neurosurgeon,' she added coyly, 'but even *I* know who you are. How on earth did you meet Suze?'

'You naughty little thing!' Louise Sadler was smiling, her beautiful aristocratic face creased with delight as she looked at Susie. 'You kept this one well hidden under your hat. I expect you were hoping to surprise us...?'

'Or maybe,' Alex inserted, 'you didn't want to say anything just in case your date didn't turn up. You must have your diary filled to overflowing, Mr Burzi...'

'Sergio, please...'

'You probably don't remember me at all, but we were at the same art gallery opening a few months ago...'

'Sergio...' Louise stepped forward, still thrilled to bits, and took his arm. 'You *must* come and meet the rest of the family. Your father is going to be *delighted*,' she whispered to Susie, who had reluctantly fallen into step as they moved towards the main party, 'that you've brought along such a *gorgeous* chap...'

'Mum...'

Too late. Events had been taken out of her hands. Or rather transferred from her hands into her family's hands—and now, as the evening progressed, everyone else's hands.

So many people had heard of him. She hadn't known him from Adam when she had plonked herself next to him uninvited because she had been on the run from her dinner companion. She hoped to God that he didn't breathe a word about *that*.

Having had him all to herself for the past few weeks, she was awestruck at the ease with which he mixed. He knew just what to say to everyone. He charmed. He was witty. He was flatteringly attentive to her. And she couldn't help but feel a treacherous burst of pride at having his arm slung over her shoulders.

Even Clarissa, who was getting steadily more tipsy as the evening wore on, and who barely had time to talk to anyone because she was so wrapped up with Thomas, dragged her to one side and told her that she wanted to hear *everything* the *very* second they were alone together once she'd returned from her honeymoon.

Under any other circumstances, Susie would have been over the moon. Had they been seriously involved, and had their relationship gone beyond sex—*had she not now been carrying his baby*—she would have been bursting with happiness and daydreaming about being the next one to walk up the aisle.

As things stood…

'Did Stanley bring you? I guess you'll be wanting to head off now…'

Most of the guests had left. Only a circle of hard-core friends, all drunk, were swaying inside the marquee with glasses in their hands.

Outside, the temperature had dropped and she hugged her pashmina around her.

Somewhere in the course of the evening Sergio's bow tie had been discarded, and she wanted to slip possessive fingers under his shirt and feel that hard, roughened chest against her skin. She itched to do it.

'You're not drinking?'

'I…I've had a headache all day,' Susie mumbled.

'What's eating you?'

'Why didn't you tell me that you were coming?'

'Not *this* again. I wanted to introduce the element of surprise—let's not breathe new life into that particular argument.'

'You don't know what you've gone and done.'

'Really? Enlighten me.'

'Now that my parents have met you…especially in the presence of every single one of my family members on my mother's side…they'll all be thinking that what we have is serious—is going somewhere…'

'I'm not responsible for what other people think.'

The cool detachment in his voice washed over her like freezing sleet, penetrating through every part of her being. 'I know you're not.'

'I'm taking it that you can't face everyone's disappointment when this is over and we part company?' he said, in the same horribly remote voice.

'My parents have had a very happy marriage. Uncle Richard and Aunt Kate the same. I come from a long line of boring, happily married people…'

'They surely can't expect you to marry the first guy you meet?'

'Of course not.'

'Then you have nothing to worry about.'

'It's not that easy, Sergio. You've got the makings of the perfect son-in-law—especially after some of the guys they've met in the past. You've come here… They'll be thinking that…'

That we're in love…because they'll want someone like you for me…

It occurred to her that she had never told him how she felt about him, never breathed a word, because she had been so sure that she could play by his rules. No wonder he was having a hard time trying to work out why she was so hot and bothered because he had shown up.

'Stop analysing everything. You're so keyed up, worrying about what other people might think, that you can't seem to see that it's *your* life at the end of the day. You live it as you see fit. If other people have other plans in mind, then tough.'

'You're so black and white.'

'Like I said, I've seen what misplaced emotion can do. I stick to what I know. It makes life a damned sight less complicated.'

'What…what was that girl like?'

She hadn't been aware that she was going to ask that question until it left her mouth and Sergio, caught on the back foot, raised his eyebrows in a perplexed, impatient frown.

'What are you talking about?'

'You once said that you're the way you are because you

had a learning curve… Who was the woman who provided the learning curve?'

'What difference does it make?'

'None. And if you don't want to talk about it, then forget I asked.'

She shrugged, started making for the kitchen door of the house, which she knew would lead to the spacious ground floor and eventually the front door and her way out—although how she was getting home she had no idea. Her ride, in the form of her parents and Alex, had gone an hour and a half ago. It would have to be another taxi.

'Where are you staying?'

'Bed and breakfast. It's in the village. A bunch of us are booked in there.'

'And I,' he said smoothly, 'am booked into the one and only five-star hotel ten miles away.'

'I'd rather not come with you…'

'Sure about that?'

And he swooped to kiss her, his tongue probing into her mouth, enveloping her in a swirl of heated responses that shook her to the core.

He did this every time. She needed to think…not say goodbye to all her thought processes and cling to him like a vine.

Yet of their own volition her arms curled round his neck and she found herself gently but efficiently propelled back until she was pressed against the wall in the deserted hallway.

'We can't… Not here…'

'Then I guess that means you'll be coming back with me…'

CHAPTER SIX

'HER NAME WAS Dominique Duval. Still is, for all I know—although who can be sure? She might have moved on to marriage number two...or three...or four by now. It's been a few years, and no one could ever accuse Dominique of being anything other than a fast worker. I met her in a club.'

'You know, you don't have to talk about this if you don't want to...'

Was she really ready to hear a story of thwarted passion? Was she ready to learn all about his one and only true love and how she'd let him down? Left him to marry someone else?

'You asked, and after more time together than I'd anticipated it's only fair that you understand why me and commitment will never have anything more than a passing acquaintance.'

'When you fall in love with someone it can be brutal when things go pear-shaped—especially if you've pinned your hopes on it working out.'

She heard a certain wistfulness in her voice and pulled herself up sharply, because the last thing she wanted was for him to guess at the depth of her feelings for him. When she told him that she was pregnant she would do so as a calm, collected adult whose only priority was to discuss technicalities and to reassure him that he could take as much or as little interest as he wanted.

'Or so I would imagine,' she added.

'I have no idea what you're talking about,' Sergio informed her. 'I was never in love with that woman. It's true she made a pass at me the first time we met, but I was involved with someone else at the time, and having fun with two women at the same time has never been my style.'

'You were never in love with her? But I thought…'

'You *assumed*—from a couple of throwaway remarks.'

'How can you have a learning curve from someone you met in a club when you never had a relationship with her? Did she try and pickpocket you?'

'My hotel. We're here.'

Susie followed the direction of his finger to see a grand country house that was lit from top to bottom. Two uniformed men stood outside, as if guarding the entrance. She knew her aunt and uncle came to this hotel on a regular basis with friends. Apparently it did a very good dinner.

'And, no…pickpockets don't engender learning curves. Dominique Duval was a nurse, and she made a pass at me because she knew who I was. I was young at the time— barely out of my teens—and from a wealthy family. My mother had died years before and my father had never remarried. I was in line to inherit his fortune, but I think she knew from the get-go that a fortune in the future was a lot less enticing than a fortune she could lay her hands on immediately. Maybe if I'd been interested she would have climbed into bed with me for the fun of it, but she had set her sights higher.'

Looking back, he had been able to make sense of the interest she had shown in his background, in his widowed father—the caring, attractive ex-nurse, with a heart full of compassion and empathy because, after all, she had seen so many hurt and lonely widowers in her line of work.

'She was a *nurse*? I thought that was a caring line of work…' She was hanging on to his every word, barely noticing the grand surroundings of the hotel, or the way the woman manning the reception desk in the early hours of the morning jumped to attention the second he strode in and then scrambled behind them as they headed straight to the bank of lifts.

'You'd think…' Sergio flicked her a wry glance. 'My first powerful lesson in never judging a book by its cover.'

'And in always assuming the worst when it comes to other people's motivations…'

'Very good.'

'What happened?'

Sergio's eyes narrowed and he shrugged. His face was hard and coldly unforgiving, even though he was recalling a past situation and not currently enduring it.

'She made sure to engineer an introduction to my father and pulled out all the right cards. She was a caring, fun girl, thirty years his junior, who could understand just what he might have been going through. She told him a life alone was no kind of life—not for a sexy silver fox like him. He was flattered. For the first time in years he decided that life was worth living after all. They were married within six months and it didn't take long before her true colours started appearing. The caring, sharing nurse became the free-spending gold-digger she had been all along—and if that wasn't enough she contrived to get my father to change his will. When he died suddenly of a heart attack pretty much everything went to her, and within five years she had managed to work her way through most of his fortune. Fortunately, he'd had the sense to leave the majority of his companies to me. She was cash-rich, with a couple of houses to spare, but she was still greedy enough to consult a lawyer, in the hope that she might get her hands on some of the companies. I spent five years batting her off until she finally gave up. Where she is now is anybody's guess.'

Susie wandered over to the chaise longue by the window and sat down, her own problems temporarily on the back burner as she worked out just how he had ended up where he had.

There was safety in a hard-boiled career woman. She thought of her own sister. Alex would never be interested in anyone's money, or in furthering herself on the back of someone else. She was fiercely independent and ambitious to get ahead under her own steam. That would be the sort of woman he would be seriously interested in. A woman who had her own life—just as he had *his* own life.

'I've seen how a person can imagine they're in love,' he continued, taking up a position on the chair facing her, his long legs stretched out in front of him, his expression cool and remorseless. 'They get swept away by emotion, lose all sense of perspective, abandon their self-control. As far as I'm concerned, that's the sort of thing that never has a good ending.'

Susie thought that he might have been describing her.

'In due course,' he drawled, 'I imagine I *will* want to settle down, but when that time comes it will be rather more of a business arrangement than a giddy loss of judgement.'

He was uneasily aware of just how fast his self-control disappeared when he was presented with her glorious body, but immediately dismissed that as a cause for concern because there was a clear line of demarcation between the physical and the emotional. On the emotional front he knew exactly where he was going, and on the physical front… Well, a little loss of self-control was perfectly acceptable…it made a great change to his usual predictable diet.

Susie heard the unmistakable clang of his boundary lines being repositioned.

Her breathing quickened and she flushed under the steady gaze of his eyes.

Why had she let herself be talked into coming back here with him? She knew why. Because she was weak and in love. Because one kiss from him could send her common sense flying in all directions. Because she was just the sort of emotional type he had told her he didn't need as a long-term investment.

'It's late.'

'So it is…' He slanted her a smile that turned her bones to jelly. 'Come here.'

'I'm not in the mood for sex.'

'No? Do you want to put that to the test?'

'We need to talk, Sergio. There are things… Well, things I need to say to you…'

Sergio frowned. Women who had a pressing need to talk rarely said anything he wanted to hear. He reminded himself that she wasn't like the other women he had dated. She talked a *lot*. She probably wanted to talk about the wedding—her parents, her sister, her huge array of cousins. It made such a change from his non-existent family, as an only child born to only children.

His face cleared and he smiled.

'Let's go to bed…'

'This isn't pillow talk.'

'Who said it was? I'm just finding it hard to keep going with the chat when we could be doing other things. Why don't you give an old man a kick and do a striptease for me…?'

'You're only thirty-two!' Her face warmed and her body was going into its usual meltdown.

Sergio grinned and remained where he was, enjoying the way he had hardened for her, enjoying the thrill of what was going to follow. Sooner or later he would move on because, as she had pointed out, *they weren't suited to one another*, but just at the moment familiarity was a long way from breeding contempt.

He tried to swallow down his dislike of her reminding him that he wasn't her type, but it nagged away like a thorn in his side he couldn't quite reach.

He stood up, strolled towards the bed, shedding his clothes en route until he was left in only his trousers, which he began to remove while she watched in her usual trance-like state of fascination.

Her body was as it always was. There were no outward signs of her pregnancy. But what would happen, she wondered, when she *did* begin to show? When her flat stomach began to go round…when her breasts grew even bigger…? What would happen to that overwhelming lust he felt for her, which was the one and only thing that kept him going?

It was just one more thought to pile on all the other thoughts that were buzzing around in her head like a swarm of bees.

For the moment…

What if this was the last time she had him—*really* had him? Because she would break the news to him in the morning and then leave, giving him time to digest the indigestible.

From that point on what they had would officially be over. Which would make right now her last chance to have him make love to her, to have him touch her and feel her and want her…

If she was a coward to be snatching it with both hands then so be it.

She followed him, kicking off her high shoes, and then stood at the side of the bed, with his deep, dark eyes on her, and performed the striptease he had asked her to do.

Sexy, erotic, sensuous… In the dark so that their bodies were shadows and angles…

She was wet for him by the time she slid under the covers. Their bodies seemed perfectly matched. She had felt comfortable with him even that very first time, and she felt so much more comfortable now.

His hands knew just where to touch, what turned her on. He nuzzled her breasts and took her nipples into his mouth in a way that sent delicious sensations zapping through her. He licked her and played with her and toyed with her… taking her to the edge before bringing her back…until her whole body was on fire.

They moved together as one, in perfect unison. He enjoyed it when she straddled him, so that her breasts hung teasingly by his mouth. When she did that she was bombarded by the dual sensations of having him suckle on her breast while he teased her below with his fingers. When she took him in her mouth she knew just how to angle her body so that he could simultaneously take her in his, suck and lick her until her clitoris could take no more, and only then, when they had enjoyed one another to the max, would he don a condom and complete her fully.

This time she didn't want their lovemaking to end. She didn't want to close her eyes and fall asleep, knowing that the morning light would bring all sorts of problems to their horizon.

'So…' Sergio nuzzled her ear.

He had long since given up his habit of abandoning the woman in his bed in favour of his computer. And he had broken with tradition by allowing her to sleep over, because his mornings were always so much more satisfying when he could wake up and make love to her.

'So…?'

'So you didn't paint the full, unexpurgated picture of your background because your high-achieving family make you feel insecure…'

'Where did *that* come from?' She rolled over onto her back and stared up at the ceiling.

'I'm a problem-solver. I like it when things add up.'

'And I'm something that needs adding up?'

'Your father told me that they pleaded with you to use their apartment in Kensington but you wouldn't. Why not?'

'Because I'm not a kid. I can stand on my own two feet.'

Even though it meant living in a cramped, disgusting hovel. He could only admire her tenacity.

'You might think that you sister has it all, but she envies you…did you know that?'

Susie swung to look at him, although in the darkness she could barely make out his expression. 'Did she tell you that?'

'She didn't have to. I could decipher it from the way she described you…free-spirited…taking each day as it comes…'

'Alex enjoys her life. She's so clever you wouldn't believe it.'

'She's also the eldest. There's a lot riding on her shoulders.'

'I never thought about it from that point of view. Maybe you're right.' She sighed. 'Who cares anyway?'

'You do.'

'I'm tired.' She made herself yawn. 'It's been a big day. I'd quite like to get some sleep now.'

Sergio cupped her breast, liking the feel of its heaviness

in the palm of his big hand. He rubbed her nipple with the abrasive pad of his thumb and felt it stiffen.

'You wanted to tell me something,' he murmured. 'What was it?'

Susie stilled. This was not the right time. When she detonated that bomb she knew that she would have to take cover.

'In the morning,' she mumbled. 'I'm way too tired to string a sentence together now...'

'Too tired to touch me?' He guided her hand to his erection and felt her whole body soften and yearn towards him.

They made love slowly, like two people dancing underwater. When she came it was a long, deep climax, and she fell asleep almost immediately, her body curled into his.

Light was streaming through the windows when she next woke, and the bed was empty. She surfaced groggily and for the first five seconds was blissfully forgetful of the daunting task that lay ahead.

Her peace of mind didn't last long and she sat up, rubbed her eyes and spotted him at the desk, working.

'What time is it?'

'After ten.'

Susie yelped and flung herself out of bed. Shower. Get cleaned up. Put her dress back on—which was going to look ridiculous at ten in the morning. And of course she had no make-up with her...not even a hairbrush.

She couldn't face having this talk until she was fully dressed. Being naked and in his bed made her vulnerable.

She locked the bathroom door. For the first time. No sexy, steamy shared shower. No touching. She wasn't even sure she would be able to look him squarely in the face, never mind having his hands on her, exploring her body, turning her brain to mush.

'Why the big rush?'

He looked at her as she emerged fully clothed from the bathroom. As jumpy as a cat on a hot tin roof. Suddenly that vague feeling was back with him—the feeling that something wasn't quite right. And yet…they had spent another incredible night together. What could be wrong? She had recovered from her little fit of pique at the thought that he had gatecrashed the wedding so that he could see for himself where she came from.

He shot her a slow, deliberate smile and it took all the will power in her repertoire not to fold.

'I'm going to call a taxi to…er…take me back to London.'

She stuck out her chin and looked at him challengingly and Sergio frowned.

'Why? Stanley's waiting. My very lucky chauffeur was treated to a night in one of the finest hotels in the county so that he could be on standby for when I was ready to leave.' He relaxed back in the chair, folded his arms on his chest and gazed at her.

'I'm going to have to detour via the bed and breakfast I was booked into…get the stuff that I left in the room… change clothes…that sort of thing…'

Sergio didn't say anything and silence filled the room, as heavy as a lead weight.

'This is beginning to get on my nerves, Susie. What exactly is it that you want to say? If it's a little speech about our future, then I'll spare you the trauma of initiating the subject. You know how I feel on the matter.'

Sudden tension lent his voice a sharp edge that made her flinch back, as if she had been struck.

'Of *course* I know!' she snapped tensely. 'You've made it perfectly clear from day one and you haven't let up since!'

Startled at her own outburst, because it was so unlike

her, she felt tears prick the back of her eyes. She blinked rapidly and took a few deep breaths. She'd been snapping at him since he had arrived and she would continue until she got what she had to say off her chest.

Sergio's jaw hardened. 'The reason I'm repeating myself,' he drawled, with just the right level of boredom to induce in her another jag of misery, 'is because weddings can sometimes do things to a girl. She sees her best friend, or in your case her cousin, walking up the aisle and suddenly she starts thinking that it's about time her turn came along.'

'I wasn't thinking that.'

'No? Because your father happened to mention in passing that a big white wedding is the only thing you've ever really wanted. Apparently you used to spend your childhood days dressing up your dolls in big wedding dresses and marrying them off to whatever stuffed toy was handy.'

Susie's cheeks flamed. She'd forgotten about that. She'd certainly never thought that her father had paid the slightest bit of attention to that phase of her life.

'I had no idea you'd been having such in-depth conversations with my parents. What else did they happen to mention "in passing"?'

'That you insisted on that secretarial course which had only ever been a suggestion. You clung to it and stuck it out—even though it was obvious from day one that you were allergic to all things technological and got bored the second you stepped foot inside an office.'

Shaking, Susie slithered towards the chaise longue and sat down, giving her wobbly legs a rest.

He had no right to just turn up and then to burrow his way into her past via her parents. Not now. Not when everything was changing.

'That's not the way I remember it...' she said, distracted. 'Alex was always the golden girl.'

'Memories can get a little distorted. The truth usually lies somewhere in the middle.'

'Well, it doesn't matter. The truth is your showing up uninvited to Clarissa's wedding…meeting my parents… wasn't a good idea.'

'Because they might get the wrong impression and think that this is more serious than it actually is…? Your mother might start shopping for a hat…? Your father will begin to prepare his father-of-the-bride speech…? You've already mentioned that. This conversation is beginning to go round in circles.'

'It's okay for you to sit there and *smirk*!' she said in a high-pitched voice. 'But you don't know what it's like!'

'And maybe you're overplaying how you think your family might respond to the fact that you're going out with me. They might, actually, be a little more pragmatic than you give them credit for… They might be just a little more realistic…' He shifted, looked at her with cool, assessing eyes. 'And since when have you taken to shouting?'

'I wasn't shouting. I was trying to make a point.' She sighed and ran her fingers through her tumbling hair. 'Maybe this is just a side to me that you haven't seen before. The shouting side.'

She wiped her perspiring hands on her dress and flopped back on the chaise longue, because her legs were beginning to come over all weak and wobbly again.

'Look…I just want you to know that I don't expect anything from you. Nothing at all.'

Sergio's eyes narrowed. He tilted his head to one side, as though listening for something only he would be able to hear.

'I'm not following you.'

Tense as a bowstring, Susie sprang to her feet and began pacing the room, her movements agitated. Every so often her eyes slid across to him—and the closed expression on his beautiful face didn't exactly fill her with confidence.

She fought against the temptation to put off this awkward conversation for another day. When she was feeling a little stronger. After she had absorbed all the ramifications of her situation for herself and rustled up some kind of plan. At which point she would be able to present him with a *fait accompli*, all-corners-covered type of situation...

'There's something you need to know...and I'm afraid it's going to put a completely different spin on what we... er...have...'

Sergio stilled. Normally so adept at reading situations, he discovered that his breathing had slowed down and his brain was not operating to its usual heightened state of efficiency.

Something was wrong. *What?* She still fancied the hell out of him. Even sitting there, barely meeting his eyes and wringing her hands, he could *sense* the mutual attraction pouring between them like a wave of electricity, undiminished.

Was she about to announce that she had done something at the wedding? While he had been busy discovering all sorts of things about her, thanks to her parents and her sister? She had seemed to know nearly every one of the guests there, including all the young men, who were obviously mutual friends of the bride and her cousins.

Jealousy rammed into him with such force that he drew his breath in sharply. Graphic images of her sneaking off with some guy behind his back competed in his head to make him feel physically sick.

Jealousy? Since when had he ever been jealous when it came to any woman?

'I'm losing patience with this long-winded non-explanation,' he said tightly, reining in unfamiliar emotions with difficulty. 'If you have something to say, then why don't you stop going round the houses and just say it?'

'I'm pregnant.'

It was the last thing he had expected to hear and so it took him a few seconds to digest the revelation.

Then he laughed mirthlessly.

'You have *got* to be kidding.'

'Do I look like someone performing a comic routine, Sergio? I'm pregnant. I only found out yesterday. I did the test. In fact I did two tests. There's no mistake. I'm having a baby. I'm having *your* baby.'

He vaulted upright, stared at her and raked his fingers through his hair. 'You *can't* be.'

He stood in front of her, feet apart, challenging her to defy that simple statement of truth.

But in his heart he recognised the ring of sincerity and fought against it.

Pregnant? How the hell had *that* happened? He was going to be *a father*? Even when he had loosely contemplated the idea of eventually settling down with a suitable woman his thoughts had not stretched into the realms of fatherhood.

His eyes flew to her stomach and just as quickly looked away.

'Don't tell me that I *can't be*,' Susie snapped.

She glared at him. Did he think she was lying? No, of course not! He was desperately clinging to denial because the alternative was so hideous that he couldn't bring himself to give it credence. He was a man who liked to control every aspect of his life, and just like that he'd lost it.

She'd gone into this with her eyes wide open, never realising that she would be playing with fire. This was what it felt like to end up loving someone who didn't actually love you back. A sick, empty feeling, as if you were spinning in a black abyss, not knowing how to get out.

But there was no point getting all worked up in the face of his reaction.

'I've worked out that it happened that first time,' she said, gathering herself. 'Yes, we were careful all the other times—but there you go. I don't see the point of wasting time trying to blame one another...'

'Who said that I was apportioning blame?'

'I wish you'd sit down, Sergio. You're not making this any easier for me. I...I'm having to take all this in myself...'

'You knew the entire time we were at the wedding?'

She nodded.

'And you said nothing to me?'

'I hardly expected you to turn up unannounced, Sergio! Besides, this isn't the sort of conversation to be had over some bubbly and canapés.'

'You *were* taken aback when I showed up...'

His brain cranked slowly back into gear. He sat down, and hunkered forward, forearms resting lightly on his thighs.

'You didn't want me to meet your parents because if I was in the picture it would be hard to eliminate me as the father. Were you planning on telling them that you were pregnant by some guy you'd met by chance?' His mouth twisted sardonically. 'Some mustard-wearing creep you met on a misguided online date, maybe?'

'No! But if you want the truth,' she told him bluntly, 'I knew it would complicate things if you were around. It's going to be horrendous enough getting through this...explaining to everyone that I'm pregnant...'

Except maybe he was right... Maybe they weren't going to be as disappointed as she had imagined—maybe they

would accept it the way they perhaps, possibly, had ac-
cepted her—and she hadn't even seen that because she'd
always been so busy comparing herself to Alex and to her
high-achieving, brilliant parents...

'And our unmarried state is going to be hard for them
to swallow, given their traditional views on life,' he said
acidly. 'Erasing me would have made a hell of a lot more
sense. You're right. Maybe you could even have made me
out to be some kind of bastard who got you pregnant and
did a runner...? The possibilities are endless, aren't they,
when it comes to disposing of an inconvenient lover...?'

'You're not being fair...'

'No?' he mocked.

'*No*. You can hardly blame me for not wanting to shout
it from the rooftops. You've made it crystal clear to me
how you feel about long-term relationships and how you
feel about *me*.'

'And how *do* I feel about you?'

'We have great sex and that's it. I get it—of course I
do. I mean...it works both ways... We've...um... Well,
I'm not about to start dumping this on you and expecting
you to do anything about it.'

Sergio banked down explosive rage.

'When you say that you don't expect me to *"do anything about it"*, what exactly do you mean?'

Her eyes flicked nervously across to him. What was he
thinking? What was going through his head? His world had
been turned upside down but at least he hadn't shouted,
or accused her of deliberately trying to pin him down.
Given his experiences with his father's second wife, he
might have.

'I mean this isn't part of your life plan,' she said. She
stared down at her clasped fingers but could still feel his
eyes pinned to her. 'And you don't have to think that you're

going to be lumbered with…with taking responsibilities you hadn't banked on. As you may have noticed, my parents are pretty well off… I'll manage financially…'

'I'm going to pretend that I didn't hear what you just said,' Sergio told her evenly. 'And I'm going to get this back on track by pointing out a few things. The first is that you don't know me at all if you think that I am the kind of man who sleeps with a woman and then walks away from a situation like this. The second is that *my* baby is *my* responsibility. I have no intention of handing that responsibility to your parents or any other member of your sprawling family, for that matter. Am I making myself clear on this?'

'That's fine,' Susie whispered. 'If you want to contribute financially, then I won't say no. I just think it's important for you to understand that—'

'You're not hearing me!'

Susie started, and stared at him nervously. 'You want to…to help out with money. I understand.'

'This is not just *your* deal. Whether I wanted this explosion in my life or not, it's happened—and I intend to be a fully committed player in the game. I'm not just going to set up a direct debit to your account and visit as and when I can… Oh, no. And if you're thinking along those lines, then you've completely misread the situation, Susie. Start the countdown, my darling. Whether either of us wants it or not, you're about to become Mrs Burzi…'

CHAPTER SEVEN

SEVERAL WORDS LODGED in Susie's head with dagger-like precision. *Explosion. Player in the game.* And finally, *Whether either of us wants it or not...Mrs Burzi....*

'We're both overwrought,' she managed in a strangled voice. 'You need a few days to take this in.'

She glanced wildly at the door and wondered whether she could make a sprint for it.

'You're not going anywhere, so you can forget eyeing the doorway like it's the promised land, and I don't need a few days to think about this. I've already thought about it and come up with the only possible solution.'

'To *marry* you? *That's* the only possible solution?'

'What else?'

The sexy, teasing man she had fallen in love with had gone. In his place was this cold-eyed stranger, addressing her in a voice that could freeze water.

'I take full responsibility for the mess we've ended up in. It's the first time I have ever come close to any kind of lapse in taking precautions.'

'You should hear yourself!'

'What are you talking about?'

'The *mess* we've ended up in...an *explosion* in your life...' Tears stung the back of her eyes. 'How can you be so...so...*callous*...?'

'I'm not being callous.' Sergio flushed darkly and continued to stare at her.

'A few hours ago,' she slammed into him bitterly, 'you were dragging me in here so that you could make love to me...'

'You weren't protesting.'

'I never said that I was!' Her eyes flared and she held his stare with mutinous, stubborn persistence.

His change should come as no big surprise. He had never been in it for more than the sex and now his true colours were showing—because whether he magnanimously chose to take responsibility or not the fact was that circumstances had changed horrendously for him.

He wasn't aiming to be callous. For him it was truly an explosion in his life—and a mess. It just wouldn't occur to him that those words would be the last ones she might want to hear.

'I don't want to get into a huge argument with you,' Susie told him wearily. 'But I'm not going to marry you. And quite honestly I have no idea why you would want to marry *me*. Especially when you had such a dramatic "learning curve", with your father marrying the wrong woman and then suffering for his mistake. Why would *you* want to marry the wrong woman?'

'Circumstances are somewhat different in our case, wouldn't you say? For a start, you aren't decades my junior, and you didn't actively seek me out so that you could extract money from me.'

'That's not what you thought when we first met! And you came here because you needed to satisfy yourself that you hadn't made a mistake. No point taking unnecessary chances.'

'It's not going to further this situation if we keep delving into the past. That's over and done with.'

'It still doesn't change the fact that I won't marry you. We're not living in the Dark Ages, Sergio. What would be the point of sacrificing our lives just because we happened to make a mistake? People make mistakes all the time, but it doesn't mean that they condemn themselves to paying for it for the rest of their lives.'

Sergio took every single word that left her mouth as a personal affront.

Marriage had not crossed his radar in any way, shape or form...*ever.* Yet he knew that had he offered what he was offering now to any of the women he had dated in the past they would have bitten his arm off in their enthusiasm to accept.

Not only had she turned him down, she had done so without a hint of apology or remorse, and she had told him in no uncertain words that he was not up to scratch, not what she was looking for.

'So tell me how *you* see this situation playing out?' His voice was icy. 'You remain living where you are? In a flat that is barely big enough for one person, far less two? With temperamental central heating and appliances that don't work unless they feel like it? Do you envisage romantic times as a pauper, having to swaddle my baby in layers of clothes or risk frostbite? Or will you take up the other option of running back home to Mummy and Daddy and living under their roof for the foreseeable future? Because—and let's be brutally honest here—your job won't pay the way.'

'I haven't thought that far ahead,' Susie said faintly. 'Of course I know that it's not going to be feasible to stay where I am...'

'So the Mummy and Daddy option will come into play. Is that it?'

'That's not what I said!'

'Then what exactly *are* you saying?'

'As you know, my parents have an apartment in London...' But she cringed at the thought of taking them up on what would be their inevitable offer. Probably not even an offer. They would *insist*.

She had spent too many years doing her best to maintain her independence, and somehow she just knew that if she caved in to parental pressure at this point—even well-intentioned parental pressure—she would fall into a trap from which it would be nigh on impossible to escape.

'Over my dead body.'

'We could work something out,' Susie muttered, staring at the ground. 'Okay, I accept that my job doesn't pay enough...isn't stable enough... And I...' She swallowed painfully as a vision of her limited options raced through her head like the steel jaws of a trap, propelling her into a place she fought hard against. 'I don't want to run crying to my parents for financial assistance. It's bad enough that they're going to try and shove it down my throat the second they hear that I'm pregnant.'

'They won't do any such thing if they're aware that you're financially being taken care of by me.'

'I don't *want* to be taken care of financially by you!' She closed her eyes, breathed deeply, opened them and stared at him without blinking. 'I might not be one of life's great financial successes but I've never wanted to rely on anyone. How do you think you're going to feel when you're stuck having to dole out money to me?'

'Don't worry about how I'm going to feel. I'm fully capable of handling my feelings. And, whether you want to rely on someone or not, you now don't have an option.'

'This isn't how I saw my life going,' Susie said quietly. 'I always thought that I would find Mr Right and everything would be done in the correct order. Love...

marriage…babies…happiness and contentment and growing old together…'

Instead, how had she ended up? Pregnant by a man who
had only ever seen her as a bit of fun—a guy who felt con-
demned to do the honourable thing and marry her for the
sake of a baby he hadn't asked for.

Sergio's jaw hardened. This was not what he wanted
to hear. Anecdotes about her ideal life weren't relevant,
given the circumstances.

'I mean,' she continued, 'what sort of life would we
have together? This was always going to fizzle out sooner
rather than later…'

There was a pause that lasted only a heartbeat as she
foolishly prayed for him to jump in and announce that that
would not necessarily have been the case. He didn't. What
had she expected?

'And now you're proposing we artificially sustain it
so that we can be shackled together. In the end, don't you
think that you'll resent me? Feel chained? Who wants to
be a prisoner of their own good intentions?'

'There's no need to be dramatic.' Sergio swept aside
her speech with an impatient wave of his hand. 'Two out
of three marriages end up in the bin, and they're generally
the ones that kick off with the starry-eyed belief that the
good times will last for ever. A union that is approached
from the point of view of a business arrangement stands
a far better chance of lasting the course.'

'And naturally this would be one of those "business arrangements"?'

'Neither of us was braced for this situation, but now that
it's occurred we can't indulge in regret and hand-wringing
and it's not helpful for you to dwell on what you would
have ideally wanted. This may come as a shock, but it's
not an ideal world.' He paused. 'There's no reason why we

can't make this work. You want to moan about chains and shackles? I don't know how many chained, shackled prisoners fall into bed with one another and make love like tomorrow may never come…'

Inappropriately, he felt himself harden. The way she dropped her eyes and licked her lips nervously only served to accelerate the surge in his libido.

Susie couldn't meet his eyes. Everything was unravelling at the speed of light and yet she couldn't help herself—couldn't turn off the full-frontal attack his proximity made on all her senses even as she resented his stupid assumption that sex might somehow make up for everything else that wasn't there. Like love.

'Why did you come back here with me?' Sergio drove on remorselessly. 'You knew you were pregnant but you didn't come back here so that you could tell me and we could talk this out…'

'I wanted… I don't know…' She backed away from an answer that would demonstrate just how powerful his effect on her was. 'I shouldn't have. I should have taken some time out to really get my head round this and then I should have approached you in a…a more neutral setting.'

'By which you mean anywhere devoid of a bed? Why don't you admit it, Susie? You came back here because you wanted to sleep with me. You wanted me to make love to you…to touch you in all those places you like being touched. Bit rich to talk about self-sacrifice and chains and shackles when you can't wait to jump into bed with me, wouldn't you agree?'

Susie squeezed her thighs tightly together. He made it sound so straightforward. A business arrangement with the added bonus of good sex.

Except she didn't *want* a business arrangement, and good sex didn't last for ever. If she married him she might get the guy she loved, but that didn't mean she would end up with the guy of her dreams because those were two completely separate issues. The man of her dreams could only ever be the man who returned her love. What she would end up with would be a nightmare from which she would never be able to escape.

She would be trapped, loving him, and her love would make her desperate and clingy and needy—just the sort of woman he would end up despising. He would find excuses to work later and later, and eventually he would end up having an affair with someone like Alex…a clever, sophisticated woman who could hold his interest once the lust had gone. She, on the other hand, would be left at home to bring up the baby. She would spend half her time crying and the other half trying to regain his attention.

'I should leave…' she breathed defiantly.

'You should be honest with yourself,' Sergio returned with equal cool speed.

There were staring at each other in this difficult situation like combatants in a ring, but he could still feel the intense electricity between them, sizzling like a live charge.

'The passion between us hasn't waned because you're carrying my baby. It's a start.'

'Passion fades—what then?'

'We're going to be having a child and I won't be a part-time father. I'm not going to let someone else enter your life and slip into the role of being the man who's there all the time, making the joint decisions, while I show up on a weekly basis trying to play catch-up.'

'It wouldn't be that way,' she said uncomfortably. When she thought about some other man coming along and sweeping her off her feet her mind went blank.

'And how are *you* going to feel down the line?'

'I don't know what you mean…' She looked at him, confused.

'When I find someone else…when she comes along with me on those weekly visits…gets to know our child, takes an interest, has input into my decision-making process…'

Susie felt the colour leave her cheeks. Of course he would find someone else. He wasn't a man who would be inclined to spend too much time celibate. He was rich beyond belief, even more powerful, and it would be a matter of seconds before he became an object of pursuit.

She imagined what this fictitious pursuer would look like and it played on all the old insecurities she had—all the feelings of inferiority that she had spent a lifetime trying to put behind her. She would be hard as nails and ready to get stuck in when it came to all sorts of decisions that were none of her business. She would be a clever, brutally tall blonde, with a razor-sharp bob and a repertoire of hard and fast notions on how to bring up other people's kids.

And she, Susie, wouldn't be able to do a thing about it. She certainly wouldn't be finding solace in the arms of another man. No, she would be lurking in front of the television with the sound down, counting the minutes until her child was returned to her.

Furthermore, even if Sergio stepped up to the plate financially—which she knew he would, however hard she objected—he would still be a billionaire, able to afford anything and everything.

She had nightmarish visions of him buying up a toy store while she hovered in the background, clutching a bag of sweets and offering a trip to the park, hoping it proved a more successful lure.

'Well?' he prompted, snapping her out of her cruel reverie. 'How is *that* scenario sounding?'

'We can come to some kind of agreement on the financial side of things. As for the rest… Sergio, I'm exhausted. I've had this shock…on top of the wedding…I'm hardly thinking straight. I feel dead on my feet.'

He looked at her, seeing the dark circles under her eyes for the first time. He shot to his feet and then screeched to a halt in front of her.

'Okay. You're right. We can carry on this conversation tomorrow. Right now I can see you probably need to…relax…'

'Relax?' Susie grimaced. 'I don't think I'll be doing any of that any time soon.'

'Come back with me,' he urged tersely. 'You can't possibly intend to return to that dump.'

'"That dump" happens to be my home.'

'Only because you're too proud. Have you ever *felt* that it's your home? Somewhere you look forward to getting back to every evening?'

No, Susie thought wearily. It was the sort of place any person would choose to avoid at all costs.

The enormity of her situation crashed over her like a tidal wave, ebbing away to leave in its wake feelings of despair and robbing her of her naturally upbeat optimism. She didn't want to return to her parents who, however hard they tried, would not be able to resist the occasional observation on the direction her life had taken.

Lord help her if they found out that Sergio, the father of her baby, had proposed marriage—had offered her all the things most women in their right minds would accept with alacrity. For them, it would be a no-brainer. They would be shocked and appalled that she had turned him down.

'That's not the point…'

'You moved there because you refused to accept help from your family, and I can understand that, but now isn't the time for your pride to dictate your actions. You don't only have yourself to consider. You have a baby to think about as well.'

'And what do you suggest? I'm not going to marry you. Sex isn't enough. Not for me.'

She wasn't going to accept his proposal, he thought. There was no way he intended to contemplate a negative response to what he wanted, but at the moment reminding her of all the benefits that came as part of the package deal if she married him wasn't going to work.

'I'll find you somewhere to live. I have a number of apartments in central London...but I'm thinking that they might be a little too close to the City for you.'

Thinking creatively and outside the box. Wasn't that his speciality? There was always more than one way to secure your catch. He lowered his eyes, inclined his head to one side and gazed thoughtfully into the distance.

'It would be a hassle for you, being in the centre of London,' he mused. 'In fact I'll bet you find it pretty hectic even being where you are—and that's away from the chaos of the City...'

'It can feel a bit overpowering sometimes.' She relaxed slightly. She didn't want to argue with him. 'I had to come to London for the work...'

'Or you would have stayed out in the country? Growing up in Yorkshire must have acclimatised you to great open spaces...'

'My parents told you where we lived?'

'It must have come up in conversation.'

'A lot seems to have "come up in conversation"...' There was resignation in her voice rather than irritation, however.

It was obvious that her family hadn't been able to be in the same space as him for longer than two seconds without divulging everything there was to divulge about her childhood. They were so desperate to hang on to the first guy she had brought home who wasn't a loser. She wondered what other little stories they had come out with… Her first steps? First words? First crush on a boy at the age of nine?

But then they had believed that Sergio was a proper boyfriend, hadn't they? Instead of a guy who wasn't into making long-term plans and certainly wasn't into love and marriage.

Sergio shrugged. 'So here's what I'm thinking…'

He leaned forward, all business now, and Susie looked back at him with guarded eyes.

'You don't want to marry me…and you're right—I can't force you. Naturally I believe that it is better for a child to have both parents, just as I believe that ours would be a union that stands every chance of working. We're physically good together, and you can't take away the fact that sex plays an intrinsic part in any relationship. However, if I cannot persuade you of that simple truth, then so be it.'

Having been on the roller-coaster ride of having him propose to her, she was now dazed at the sudden turn the ride had taken—and, if she was being honest, a little taken aback.

So much for his enthusiastic proposal. It hadn't taken him long to fall in line with what she had said—that marriage would be a ridiculous sacrifice, way beyond the bounds of duty. Why didn't she feel happier?

'I'm glad you see where I'm coming from…'

'I see it,' he murmured. *I just don't accept it.* 'But back to what I was talking about…'

She focused, even though her mind was still whirring on a different plane.

'I intend to find you somewhere a little further out.' He raised his hand, as though predicting an interruption. 'Still accessible to central London, but with more of a country feel. Richmond… Yes… Somewhere like that would do very nicely. Naturally you would want somewhere to carry on painting? That's the good thing about what you do—you can work from the comfort of your home. No nasty commuter trips into London.'

'You're going to rent somewhere for me?'

'Buy,' he corrected. 'I've always thought that renting is the equivalent of throwing money down the drain. And,' he carried on quickly, because he could glimpse her pride beginning to make an unwelcome appearance, 'it won't just be for *you*. It will be for you and our child. It won't be big or spectacular, so you needn't start trying to put boundaries around what would and wouldn't be acceptable to you.'

'I wasn't about to do that.' Susie blushed and looked away. He knew her so well that it was scary. 'Am I allowed to have a say in this house? Or do I get presented with it as a *fait accompli*?'

'It'll be a joint decision…what else?'

And in the meantime he was allowing her to carry on living in her little rented hovel.

Now that she was pregnant Susie realised just how awful a place it was. As a young, single person, she could weather all the drawbacks, but when she thought of bringing a newborn to the place she shuddered.

In the end she flitted between her parents' house in Yorkshire and her London apartment. They had taken the news better than she had hoped—and, after what Sergio had said to her about misreading some of their reactions in the past, putting her own personal spin on situations that only existed in her head, she was accepting of that. She didn't try to probe behind what they said, looking for hidden depths and meanings that weren't there. She didn't try to open up any cans of worms.

Besides, she didn't seem to have the luxury of time on her hands to question and analyse and jump to conclusions.

She was busy looking for somewhere else to live and finding nothing. Busy trying to work out how her life was going to pan out with Sergio as a permanent part of it, but without the solid bond of marriage to glue them together. Trying to come to terms with the choices she had made because they were good choices.

He spoke to her every day, and usually several times. He insisted on visiting her at her place and made absolutely no move to try and coerce her into moving in with him. He respected her decision to take herself off to Yorkshire at a moment's notice. If he resented her decision not to tell her parents that he had proposed, then he hid it well. He was a man who wasn't emotionally involved—just doing the right thing because he had no choice.

And he kept his distance.

For the past seven weeks—ever since she had broken the news to him—he had not made any effort to touch her…except occasionally, in passing, the brush of his hand on her arm, his finger wiping something from the side of her mouth…little passing touches that sent her blood pressure into orbit and made her realise, with something bordering on utter misery, that she was the only one affected.

She didn't even know what he did and with whom when she wasn't around—when she was in Yorkshire, or back in her dingy flat trying to get her head round doing the illustrations for a job for which she had now been commissioned.

And of course she couldn't ask, could she? She had taken their relationship to the level of business and he had fallen in. He was doing just what she had told him was acceptable—contributing financially and, frankly, being morally supportive—taking her out for the occasional meal, and once actually cooking something for her at her flat when she hadn't felt like eating out. It had been a charade of domesticity that had cut her to the quick.

She had laid down her boundaries and he was simply respecting them.

So asking him if he was seeing anyone was totally out of the question.

But she wondered. He no longer wanted her. That physical urgency had disappeared. She thought that her changing body probably didn't help.

She was still wondering now, as she stepped off the train onto a packed platform bustling with tourists and people going who knew where?

Spring had morphed into a lovely summer. Having had no morning sickness to speak off, she was now finding the hotter weather more difficult to deal with. She felt tired most of the time. Her breasts had shot up by two whole sizes and she hadn't been exactly flat-chested to start with.

She had turned into a beach ball.

Suddenly demoralised, she dragged her pull-along case through the crowds, bumping into people and vaguely apologising while her thoughts whirled between Sergio and what he was doing, and with whom, and how she would react when she found out.

The glare of the sun was strong outside and she shaded her eyes for a few seconds, getting her bearings, pleased that she had decided to opt for a taxi rather than the Underground. She felt exhausted. Her parents, who now seemed to be around all the time, where before they had always been jetting off to some glamour spot or another, had fussed around her, trying their best to feed her up.

'First grandchild for the Thornton line!' Susie had heard her mother trill merrily down the line when she had been talking to her sister, Kate.

She was still away in her own little world, dragging her feet to the taxi rank, when she felt a hand on her shoulder. She jumped and spun round, to find herself looking straight into Sergio's dark sunglasses.

All at once her heart began to beat wildly and her body did all those things she was always telling it not to do whenever she was with him. Her pulses raced, her mouth went dry, her nervous system threatened to go into meltdown.

'What are you doing here?'

'I've come to collect you.' He nodded to where Stanley was parked illegally by the kerb and simultaneously removed her bag from her clutches. 'At least you've listened to me and decided against battling on the Underground, but I still think you should let Stanley drive you up when you want to visit your parents.'

She smelled of the sun and the countryside. He occasionally suspected that it was a smell he had become accustomed to because it seemed to follow him everywhere he went.

'I might be pregnant but I can still travel very well by myself. Besides, it's more convenient to get there on the train.'

When she had first discovered that she was pregnant and contemplated how he might react to the news she had foreseen a lot of things—but she hadn't foreseen that he would rein in his natural need to control everything, to be the winner in the game…that he would bend to what she wanted.

He was considerate and he was nice. And the nicer he was, the more churlish she felt, and she had to stifle the inappropriate thought that she didn't want *nice,* she wanted *passionate.*

He was being *nice* now, and all she wanted was to fling

herself at him and feel those sexy, sensuous lips on her, feel his hands on her body. She missed that so much.

She stole a sidelong look at his clean, strong, chiselled profile and the sweep of raven-black hair combed away from his face. The sunglasses were still on and she couldn't read the expression on his face.

She brushed past him, settling herself into the back seat of the car, and began chatting to Stanley, with whom she had struck up a pleasant friendship over the time she had known him. His two loves in life were cars and baking, and he began telling her about a new recipe he had tried for ciabatta bread.

'Pipe down, Stanley,' Sergio ordered. 'How many times…?'

'There's some folk who are actually *interested* in what I have to say…sir!'

Sergio sighed heavily and his eyebrows shot up, but he didn't prolong the conversation, instead smartly shutting the glass partition so that they were enclosed in a private cocoon in the back of the car.

'That was very rude.' Susie sat back and closed her eyes to block him out, but she was keenly aware of him with every pore in her body.

'Stanley would be shocked if I was ever anything but. As a matter of fact there's a reason why I showed up here to collect you, Susie.'

She turned to look at him, suddenly nervous. 'What is it?'

Was he about to tell her that she had been replaced? That he was seeing someone else but not to worry, because he would still make sure she was financially taken care of…still make sure that he kept showing up to offer her support…because she was, after all, *carrying his child*.

A fact which he seemed to have taken on board with

effortless ease. Although for all she knew he might spend every second on his own cursing the day he had invited her to sit at his table so that she could escape the horror of her blind date.

'I have a surprise for you,' he drawled, leaning against the car door.

'I don't like surprises. In fact I hate them.'

'You're going to like this one.' He held her eyes steadily and smiled. 'You're now the proud owner of a house in Richmond—within spitting distance of the park…'

'What?'

'It's time you cleared out of that hovel,' Sergio told her bluntly, 'and you've spent the past two months getting nowhere very fast.'

'So you went behind my back and just…*picked some random place to speed things up*?'

'I accelerated a process that wasn't getting anywhere.'

'And when did this process of *acceleration* begin, exactly?'

'I spotted it a while back but it wasn't yet destined for the market.'

'What does that mean?'

'It means I made the owners an offer they found difficult to refuse, but I didn't want to say anything because they could have backed out at any given moment.'

'And now?'

'And now, like I said, you own a house.'

'You should have told me. You can't just make big decisions like that without consulting me! I'll probably hate it—what then?' She was being horribly unfair, but he made her feel like a parcel in need of urgent delivery. He was just so…*controlled and efficient*…

'If you do,' Sergio said with infuriating calm, 'we'll cross that bridge when we get to it. And in the meantime…'

'In the meantime…*what*?'

'Try not seeing all the negatives.'

Left to her own devices, he wouldn't have put it past her to dig her heels in, deliberately finding nothing so that she could head up to Yorkshire, far away from him and his intervention.

And he wasn't having that. Oh, no. There was no way he was going to let her run away from him…

CHAPTER EIGHT

'How are your parents?'

Sergio had seen them only once since the wedding. They had come down to London before leaving to go to Tuscany for two weeks. He had taken them out to the restaurant he owned—the very same restaurant where he had met their daughter. He had wined and dined them and no mention had been made of where he was going with Susie. With that well-bred reticence so typical of the upper classes they had steered diplomatically clear of any contentious subjects.

'Fine.'

'Have you mentioned our financial arrangements to them?'

'I've said that you won't be doing a runner,' Susie told him vaguely.

Sergio frowned. 'That's not really good enough, is it?'

'They understand that just because I'm pregnant it doesn't mean that we're going to be walking up the aisle.'

'Even though I expect that is what they would like to see?'

She shrugged and held his stare. 'I haven't gone into lots of detail, but I think they understand that in this day and age people don't get married because of an accidental pregnancy. They know that you're…you're…'

'Not going to leave you in the lurch. But you haven't mentioned the fact that you'll be getting a house?'

'I've said that I'm looking for somewhere more suitable to live once the baby's born. They offered to get me somewhere, but I told them that you were insistent on getting involved in the financial side, so you needn't worry that they don't see you as a responsible person. They do.'

'And I take it you haven't mentioned that I asked you to marry me?'

'Why would I do that when we're not going to be married?'

It was the first time he had raised the subject for several weeks, and she wondered where she would be now if she had accepted his proposal. Would she now be Mrs Susannah Burzi? It was unfairly alluring and she pushed the thought aside—because if you weren't embarking on a life of at least *hopefully* happily married bliss, then what was the point? She could never, *would* never, see marriage as a convenient arrangement.

Furthermore, she was still simmering at the thought of a house being bought behind her back, and was gearing up to finding fault—because what did *he* know about her tastes when it came to houses? He had only ever seen her in her 'rented hovel', as he liked to call it. His own apartment was the height of what money could buy, but it wasn't the sort of thing she personally liked. Too clinical, too lacking in atmosphere.

She envisaged somewhere smart and modern…maybe in a discreetly upmarket estate.

Sergio didn't say anything. With every passing day he could feel her withdrawal. The fire that had raged between them still managed to keep him up at night, but for her it was gradually being snuffed out—overtaken by events that neither of them had anticipated.

Occasionally, yes, he could feel the heat emanating from her, but often, like now, he could sense her blocking him out. More than anything else he wanted to shake her out of her retreat and return her to the land of the living—which included *him*.

Right now her profile was averted, her mouth set in a tight line. He fancied she might be silently cursing him for having found somewhere for her to live, thereby removing all possibility of her returning to the wilds of Yorkshire to take up residence on her parents' sprawling country estate.

If they had given her a hard time things might have been slightly different, but they hadn't. He had known from the very first second he had been introduced to Louise and Robert Sadler that their youngest daughter's driving need to please them, her keen sense of being the least able of the crew, the one doomed to disappoint, was largely in her imagination.

She had grown up in the shadow of her enormously academic sister, and both her parents had likewise been hugely academic, gifted in their separate fields. From there had sprung Susie's oversensitivity—which, in turn, had led her to misinterpret things her parents might have said in the past.

In fact they had absorbed the whole pregnancy deal with aplomb.

Hence he knew that whereas before she might have hesitated to ask for their help, things had subtly changed, and the lure of Yorkshire was a very real threat to his plans to get her to remain as close to him as possible.

He had debated informing her parents that he had proposed, and thereby really throwing the cat among the pigeons, but had regretfully discarded that option—because forcing a woman to do something she didn't want to do would bring cheaply won and very short-lived success.

He might enjoy controlling situations, but he drew the line at being a complete fool.

'You *could* make an effort to *not* look as though you're being led to a torture chamber,' he said drily, and Susie, who had been staring through the window, turned to look at him.

She wondered if the day would ever come when she would be able to look at him without melting inside. Probably not. And in the meantime the only thing that helped was to avoid looking at him as much as possible.

'Sorry. I was miles away.'

'Thinking about what?'

'Just about the illustration I'm doing at the moment,' she lied. 'It's very intricate.'

Sergio thought that there was no reason for her to be hunched over an easel, working away at something that from what he could tell paid peanuts in the big scheme of things, but he kept that to himself.

'No interest in hearing what the house is like?' He tried to keep the annoyance out of his voice.

'It's not going to make any difference, is it?' she pointed out politely. 'Considering it's already been bought.' She sighed and ran her fingers through her hair, untangling small knots. 'I know I should be grateful. You've been very good over all this. There are a lot of guys who would have been running for the hills a long time ago.'

'And there are some who might have tried to force your hand when it came to the marriage situation,' Sergio countered.

'I suppose… Not that you can force someone to do something they don't want to do.'

'You'd be surprised how many men might dislike the thought of their child being born out of wedlock.' His voice was grim.

'That's such an old-fashioned expression.'

But she didn't like the thought of any child starting life on a conveyor belt, being shuffled between parents. Would she be blamed in the years to come? Would she end up being the villain in the piece? Her conscience stirred uneasily.

'And it's better than a child being torn apart between two warring, unhappy parents. Where are we?'

Busy streets had given way to more open spaces. The houses were spaced further apart. Up ahead she saw open fields and she sat forward, peering ahead.

'Richmond Park stretches for miles around,' he said, grimly and silently contemplating the reality that she saw any union between them as a potential battleground.

Susie was enchanted. You could almost forget that London was still accessible. She had been to a couple of parks, but generally the ones she had been to had been small and crowded. This stretched as far as the eye could see—a wilderness and yet still attached to the most vibrant city on the planet.

The car had slowed, was now manoeuvring through a series of roads that became smaller and smaller, until eventually they pulled up in front of a house that sat squarely in the middle of a well-tended garden.

'We're here,' Sergio said, swinging out of the car as it pulled to a stop.

'It's…amazing…'

'You sound shocked. What were you expecting? A smaller version of my apartment? No, don't bother answering that. I can tell from the expression on your face that you were.'

He had the front door key, but first he wanted to show her the garden. They walked to the side and he led her to the back of the house, which was even more picture-perfect than the front. Overlooking the extensive open land of the park, the house gave an illusion of isolation that was seductive.

Fruit trees bordered a small, containable garden, in which a bench had been cleverly positioned so that the occupant would have unparalleled views of the parkland.

On cue, Susie strolled over and sat down.

'It's a little chilly out here,' Sergio said after a few minutes. 'Let's go inside. You can see the rest of the house.'

She followed him and everything inside seduced her—from the cosy kitchen with its bottle-green Aga, to the quaint arrangement of rooms downstairs, each with its own personality but all of them warm and inviting.

'Does this furniture belong to the owners?' She ran her hands along the back of a sofa which was upholstered in colours of faded rose and cream.

'No. I had it fully kitted out when the sale went through.'

Susie yanked her hand back as though it had been stung by a wasp. 'So you chose the house and you chose the furniture as well?'

'Do you like it?'

'That's not the point.'

'Then what, exactly, is the point?'

He moved towards her and she stumbled a couple of paces back.

'How long do you intend to maintain silent warfare between us, Susie? If that's your way of trying to get rid of me through the back door, then rest assured that it's not going to work.'

Susie licked her lips. In a desperate attempt not to find herself staring at him she turned her head. He firmly redirected it by dint of one finger on her chin.

'I'm not... I... There's no warfare between us...'

But that was how he would interpret her attempts to

detach herself from him, even though they still gelled, still talked to one another…even though, when her guard was down, she always seemed to fall right back into him, enjoying his wit, his humour and his sharp, invigorating intelligence.

Their eyes tangled and hers dipped involuntarily to his mouth. She heard and felt the sharp intake of his breath and pulled back, heart beating fast.

For a second there…

If he touched her she didn't know what she would do. She suspected the worst. She dreamt of his hands on her body and his mouth on hers. But everything was different now, and she refused to let herself slip back into letting her body rule her head.

'I love all the stuff, Sergio,' she said, regaining her composure and moving to admire one of the table lamps. 'The colours are perfect. Very warm. Just my kind of style.'

Sergio, who was busy trying to subdue the sort of erection that ached to be touched, barely heard her.

'Upstairs.' His voice was harsher than he'd intended. 'A quick look round and then we can leave. I have the keys and the house is ready for you to move in whenever you are.'

Susie took the hint. Whatever charge had sprung up between them it was one he wanted to kill as thoroughly as she did. Thinking that did something to her, made her feel sick, and she darted up the stairs, slowing down to take in all the bedrooms. Four of them. And at the very end…

She stopped dead in her tracks and gazed in wonder at the studio which overlooked the back garden and through which streamed light from windows that covered the expanse of nearly one wall.

'Will it do?'

She turned to him and smiled shyly. 'I have a *studio*…'

She explored every glorious inch of it while he stood by the door, his dark eyes following her every small movement. She loved the house but here, in this studio, she was like a kid in a candy shop.

'The light's absolutely perfect,' she enthused, pausing to admire just how perfect it was by standing and staring out of the window. 'And the workbench…the double sink…' She admired both for a while. 'I can put my easel just there…I won't have to sit at that awful table with a light next to me, trying to get the colours right…'

'Bad for a pregnant woman,' Sergio agreed gruffly.

They'd been politely circling one another for so long now that he hadn't realised how much he missed seeing her truly relaxed. He'd never wanted to kiss her as much as he did just at that moment. He was sick to death of being the good guy. He knew what the outcome of this situation should be and waiting to get there involved depths of patience he had never known he possessed.

She walked towards him and flung her arms around him in a hug.

A hug. He didn't want a *hug*. He gently disengaged her, because if she pressed herself any closer to him he knew that he wouldn't be responsible for what happened next. Just as he knew that *what happened next* would shatter the fragile relationship between them and send her on the first train back to Yorkshire.

Which was something he wasn't going to allow.

He was playing a waiting game, and it was a game at which he had next to no experience. He was a man who got what he wanted, and gently going down different paths and exploring different avenues to get there was unheard of.

But it would be worth it.

She was having his baby, and she wasn't going to disappear halfway up the country to bring it up without his

input. He had no doubt that should she do that it wouldn't
be long before some man took an interest in her. She would
be a mother, but she would also be so damned sexy that
she took your breath away.

And in her search for Mr Right she wouldn't be inclined
to slam the door shut on any hopefuls, would she?

'Yes. It is.'

Embarrassed at her enthusiastic response, which had not
been returned, Susie exited the room with a final back-
ward glance.

The atmosphere had changed. How, she couldn't quite
put her finger on. She just knew that something had sprung
up between them that threatened the control she had been
working so hard to establish.

'I take it you don't loathe it, the way you assumed you
would?' This as they were back in the car, heading away
from the house.

'I thought it was going to be like your apartment.'

'You're telling me that you loathe my apartment?' He
kept his tone light but it was an effort.

'It's very, very impressive, but the more time I spent in
it the more cold and clinical I found it…'

'I had an interior designer take care of everything and
it works for me. I'm seldom there.'

'So who took care of furnishing the house?' Susie asked
curiously.

Sergio flushed. 'Someone else.'

'And you…supervised the whole thing?'

'I had some input, yes.'

Startled, she said, 'I can't picture you going to a fabric
shop and choosing what colour you wanted the curtains to
be…or having a browse in a sofa shop for the right sofa…
It used to take a lot of effort just getting you down to the
local supermarket…'

'But you have to admit,' Sergio drawled, 'that once I was there I was excellent when it came to getting what was needed.'

'You were *terrible*. You never got anything that was actually necessary. You were always intrigued by weird ingredients and bright packaging. Like a kid.'

Had they reached that level of domesticity? How had that happened? When? How was it that he hadn't noticed?

She hastily changed the subject. 'I shall have to have a look around at the local shops. See what's there and how I can get to them on public transport.'

'Which brings me to the matter of you hopping on and off the tube or trying to hunt down a bus in winter. It doesn't work.'

'You mean I won't be accessible by public transport?' Susie asked, dismayed.

'I mean I'm going to get you a car—and before you launch into a long speech about not needing one, you do, and the subject is non-negotiable. This is about doing what's right for the woman who happens to be carrying my baby. To be blunt, the hassle of the Underground, the walk in winter to get there or to get to the nearest bus stop, and then the jostling, the crowds…unacceptable. You just need to decide what kind of car you want.'

'A top-of-the-range Lamborghini…' Susie said through gritted teeth.

Sergio burst out laughing. 'Colour?'

'I was joking.'

'I wouldn't have got you one. Impractical. If I'm in it with you, where would the baby go? On the roof?'

'I actually hadn't anticipated you being a passenger in my car,' she said tersely, eyes narrowed at the grin still tugging at the corners of his mouth. 'Why would I be giving you a ride somewhere?'

'Who knows?' He gave one of those elegant gestures that were so typically foreign, so typically *him*. 'What if you suddenly decide that you want company at a supermarket?'

'That won't be happening!' *And stop playing with me!*

She pictured them browsing the aisles while he flung in exotic stuff that she instantly removed and returned to the shelves. Her heart twisted. Somewhere deep inside her she wondered whether she had been lulled into imagining that he felt more than just lust for her because she had had those little glimpses of pure happiness…

For him, it had stemmed from nothing more significant than the fact that he wanted her in his bed, and if the occasional supermarket shop came as part of the deal then he would oblige.

While for her those little things had been the building blocks cementing a relationship that had taken over her life.

'I suppose a car would be useful,' she conceded—partly because it was true, but mostly because she knew that he would end up getting his own way on this score anyway. 'But something small and second-hand.'

'I don't do second-hand.'

This elicited a snort from Stanley in the front, and Sergio immediately slid the glass partition shut—though only after he had told his driver to concentrate on what he was being paid to do instead of eavesdropping. 'But I can do small.' He looked at his watch. 'And there's no time like the present.'

'You're going to buy me a car *today*?'

'What's the point in putting it off? The house is ready. You can move in tomorrow if you choose. You'll need a car as soon as you're installed.'

By six that evening she was the owner of a brand-new shiny black five-door hatchback. A top-of-the-range, all-dancing, all-singing hatchback, fully loaded with every-thing from satnav to air conditioning.

'A house and a car,' she admitted to her mother as she lay curled up on the saggy sofa in the depressing little room which she and Sergio had jointly agreed she would vacate the following day.

'How very decent of him,' Louise Sadler said, in her usual understated manner. 'I somehow got the impression that he was prepared to support you financially, but personally finding a house he thought you would like…'

'It's nothing at all like that, Mother,' Susie rushed in hastily.

To the outsider it might seem beyond the call of duty, but she knew better. She had seen just how overwhelm-ingly obliging he could be when something was person-ally at stake for him.

Supermarket shopping, which he loathed, to placate her because he wanted her in his bed.

A house he knew she would like because she was having his baby, and there was no way he was going to let her remain in the hovel or, worse, retreat up to Yorkshire, miles away from his sphere of influence. Not with his child. No way.

'The car—yes, I can fully understand that, darling. You really would need something to get around in. But you're telling me that he chose all the fittings for this dream house of yours…?'

'He *employed* someone to choose all the fittings. He just gave them some vague idea and allowed them to run with it. You can do that when money is no object. And I never said that it was my *dream house*,' she pointed out, gazing at the keys to the house, which lay on the sofa next to her. 'My *dream house* would never be in London.'

'Well, he's been very perceptive, managing to locate something in London that gets close…'

'Luck.'

'It took Daddy and I ages to find the flat…'

'We don't have the sort of relationship where he pops down to the estate agency so that he can sit with them and look through glossy brochures of houses for me,' Susie said heavily.

She felt that it was time to address certain assumptions before they could blossom into huge inaccuracies.

'Sergio and I had lots of fun, Mother, but it would have fizzled out if this…this situation hadn't occurred…'

There was a telling silence down the line and old feelings of being a let-down, a crashing disappointment, swept over her—even though she had had a chance to re-evaluate the accuracy of those feelings. Old habits died hard, she thought, chewing her lip and waiting for her mother to break the awkward silence.

'That's how it is these days,' said Louise Sadler eventually, and sighed. 'Nothing's perfect, my darling. As long as *you* feel able to cope as a single mother, then that's the main thing.'

'You mean it, Mum?'

'I most certainly do. I…*we*…are very proud of you and the way you're handling this unexpected situation. You've been plucky and strong. You're a little soldier.'

'I am?'

'Of course you are,' her mother asserted briskly. 'You've put your heart and soul into doing what you wanted to do, you haven't accepted any help from either me or your father, and you're soldiering on…working…making sure you maintain your independence. I'll wager you're not accepting anything from Sergio without a fight.'

Susie laughed, feeling on a high. 'I make noises,' she confessed. 'You know it sticks in my throat having to accept his help. But if Sergio decides to do something it's impossible trying to stop him. Honestly, he's the human equivalent of a steamroller!'

'Quite…' her mother said after a pause. 'I expect it's what you need to be if you're to reach the giddy heights that he has…'

Buoyed by her conversation with her mother, Susie had a good night's sleep and awoke the following morning to the insistent ring of her doorbell.

She didn't bother to check the time. Instead she dragged herself out of bed and padded to the door, flinging on a dressing gown over the nightie that clung to her newly rounded body.

She pulled open the front door and there he was, in all his drop-dead gorgeous, magnificent glory, finger poised to ring the bell one more time.

She yawned. 'What time is it?'

Still drowsy, Susie swept her hand through her tangled hair and stared at Sergio, who looked unfairly bright-eyed and bushy-tailed while she felt as though she still needed a few more hours' sleep in order to face the day.

'Gone nine-thirty. Have you forgotten that you're moving in to the house today?'

His voice sounded normal, but Sergio was feeling far from normal. He had seen the change in her body only through layers of baggy clothes. Now she was standing in front of him, flimsy bathrobe hanging open, and an even flimsier nightdress revealing everything he had not been able to see properly before.

Lust hit him hard, knocking him for six. Her belly was rounded, her breasts fuller, and through the thin fabric he could easily glimpse the outline of her nipples, bigger and darker, poking against the cotton.

He discovered that his breathing was laboured. He wanted to shut the door behind him and propel her to her bed and...*take her.* It was a primitive caveman instinct that was unlike anything he had ever felt in his life before. The desire for possession roared through him and he raked his fingers through his hair and shifted restlessly on his feet.

He had to look away.

'I hope this isn't the way you answer the door to whoever happens to ring your doorbell,' he muttered hoarsely. 'You need to cover yourself up.'

Or he'd have to excuse himself to use her bathroom, so that he could relieve himself of his massive, throbbing erection.

That was like a bucket of cold water being poured over her and Susie woke up fully, recognising her state of undress and yanking her dressing gown tightly around her.

She hadn't thought! She'd been so sleepy that it hadn't occurred to her that she was on show—in all her new body glory! And judging from his reaction he couldn't have been less turned on by the sight.

Mortified, she stepped back to let him pass and excused herself hurriedly so that she could change.

She flung on anything—baggy jogging bottoms and a loose sweater with a vest underneath, warm socks and her trainers—and reappeared to find him staring through the window.

'I'm sorry.' She was tense as he slowly turned round to look at her. 'I overslept. I planned on setting the alarm but I must have forgotten... I seem to spend half my life forgetting things these days!'

She could feel the tension in the air between them and wanted to tell him that he could relax, that she wasn't about to jump on him.

Sergio was having difficulty getting words out. 'No problem.'

'I did manage to pack *some* stuff,' she continued into

the awkward thick silence. 'Not that there's that much to pack... I have a suitcase filled with clothes, but I think I might just leave my bits and pieces of crockery here. No point taking them, is there?'

Silence.

'Are you...all right? You look a bit pale.'

'We should go—get you in. You can have the day then... to settle in. I...I've made sure that there's food...some basics...' He had become a stuttering idiot. He rubbed the back of his neck.

'You—you shouldn't have,' Susie stammered.

'It's no big deal.'

Sergio recovered his composure slowly. The good news was that breathing was now possible.

'You need to rest. You can't be hopping into a car every two seconds to go down to the shops.'

He grabbed the case on the floor and gave a cursory glance round the room, which looked even more dilapidated now, if that was possible.

'I'm thinking you should paint until you feel tired, then rest.'

'I'll be the size of a beached whale if I do that. A pregnant woman needs a little exercise or else the pounds pile on.'

He didn't say anything, but from where he was standing the piling on of the pounds seemed to be increasing her sexiness—not diminishing it.

Now that she knew where they were heading Susie took the time to appreciate the joy of getting out of the packed streets and never-ending noise.

For once, Stanley wasn't driving.

'A week's holiday doing a baking course in Devon,' Sergio explained. 'The man never fails to amaze me. He's moved effortlessly from a life of breaking into cars to a life of breaking into recipe books.'

Because he had you as his mentor, was the thought that sprang instantly into her head.

The house was as delightful second time round as it had been the first time. More so, if anything. The garden seemed bigger, more abundantly landscaped, and as she stepped into the house the furnishings that she had skimmed over in her confusion at being there were more homely, warmer, more welcoming than she remembered.

He hadn't been lying when he had said that some shopping had been done. The cupboards were full—as was the fridge.

'I'll send my man back to your house to get the rest of your things.'

'There's nothing, really. Like I said, I've packed my clothes and my art stuff...and the few knick-knacks my parents gave me to make the place a little less... What's left are just some stupid posters and bric-a-brac I bought to make the place less...less...'

'Vile? Disgusting?'

The corners of her mouth twitched and unconsciously she placed her hand on her stomach. 'Maybe...'

He knew those knick-knacks. They were the anomalies in her flat that had first made him suspect her of not being who she said she was—the expensive little things that had seemed to prove her a liar, the lingering question mark that had finally driven him to that wedding.

'Why don't you stay...have something to eat...some lunch...? I mean, you've stocked the cupboards...it's only fair... Of course you must be busy... In which case...'

She met his gaze and instantly her body sprang into life. Her nipples tightened into aching peaks, her legs turned to jelly and a deep pain began in her pelvis...spreading until she was melting. He was looking at her with such intensity...

Giddy, she leaned against the wall, as weak as a kitten.

'You don't want me to stay, Susie.'

'What are you talking about? I just asked you, didn't I?'

Very slowly he walked towards her, and the closer he got the more helpless she felt.

'If I stay…I'm going to have to touch you…'

'What do you mean?' She hated herself for asking that, because the answer was written in the intensity of his gaze.

'You've changed… Your breasts have become bigger…'

'It's the pregnancy,' she said weakly.

Dangerous conversation. It played to her weakness and she knew she should resist, should say something funny or sarcastic, but all she could think was, *God, you're beautiful, and I want to make love to you more than anything else in the whole world…*

Looking at her, Sergio knew that he could have her. Right now, right here. Hell, they probably wouldn't even be able to make it up the stairs. But what would that prove? *Nothing.* And what would follow in the aftermath of that?

Marriage might be out of the question, but was he going to blow their fragile truce by stampeding her into bed like someone who had zero control? He had built his life on control, and he knew it was the most powerful ally anyone could have.

But, God, his whole body was aching. He wanted to reach out and slip his hand under the jumper, wanted to feel the weight of her breasts, wanted to push that jumper up and suckle on engorged, enlarged nipples, bigger and darker now that she was pregnant.

And he wanted to taste her down there, get his fill of her, and then come inside her without the nuisance of protection.

'I won't stay for anything,' he said abruptly. 'I should go. Is there anything else you need?'

Her body cooled and she stiffened in receipt of a rebuttal he wasn't even bothering to dress up.

'Nothing. And you're right. Silly of me to have asked you to stay. You're right—so right... You should head off...'

CHAPTER NINE

SUSIE'S FIRST THOUGHT when she felt a cramping in her stomach was to ignore it. Firstly, she didn't want to overreact and be labelled a hysterical hypochondriac by the hospital into which she had been booked. Secondly, Sergio had just left and she didn't want to summon him back on what would probably be a fool's errand.

Things had been ticking along between the two of them for the past four months.

The bigger she'd grown, the more she had tried to hide her body under an ever-changing assortment of shapeless clothes. He had rebuffed her that one time, and she wasn't going to risk falling into the trap of thinking that he might still find her sexy. He didn't. Somehow wearing attractive maternity clothes or, worse, non-maternity clothes with a high, stretchy Lycra content, would have made her feel vulnerable. She didn't want to feel vulnerable. Not on top of everything else she was having to deal with—namely the fact that her feelings towards him hadn't lessened in the slightest over time.

He wasn't around all the time, but he was around too much. He telephoned her every day without fail. She assumed to make sure that she hadn't fallen down the stairs in a state of pregnant idiocy. And he showed up every weekend, and usually once or twice during the week.

Sometimes just for a cup of coffee, and to make sure that everything was working properly in the house. Occasionally he swept aside her objections and made her go out with him for a meal.

Every second in his presence was sweet torture. She wanted to step back, had braced herself with little lectures on the healing aspect of his frequent visits, told herself that the more she saw him the easier it would get to be in his company without feeling the need to find some smelling salts just in case she came over dizzy and passed out.

But none of her mini-lectures had worked and she was just as susceptible to his presence as she had been from the very first second she had laid eyes on him.

While he… He did everything befitting a man whose sole concern was the welfare of his unborn baby.

He had made sure to employ a gardener, so that she wouldn't have to do anything remotely manual for herself outside, even though she'd tried to tell him that it wasn't necessary. He roamed through the house, making sure that everything was working, that no lights needed changing—presumably because the thought of her actually getting onto a ladder to change a lightbulb was far too risky.

He treated her like delicate porcelain and she hated it—because it was a parody of domesticity when she yearned for the real thing. She longed for the days when he hadn't been able to look at her without wanting her…when he hadn't been able to be in the same room as her without touching her, and when the sight of a bed had always led to a passionate, inevitable outcome. She wanted his attentiveness to be *for her,* and not just because she was a vessel for his baby.

Her whole body yearned for his touch. She couldn't imagine how much of a turn-off she must be for him now, with her prominent belly and her pregnant waddle, and her assortment of unappealing clothes which, as the weather had become increasingly colder with the approach of winter, were all in various shades of black or grey.

And she still wondered whether there was another woman in his life—some frisky lawyer he was keeping under wraps because he didn't want to unsettle her.

Wild horses wouldn't have dragged the question out of her. She wasn't sure whether it was because there was no way she would let him see just how deeply her feelings for him ran, like an underground torrent waiting to burst through given the slightest opportunity, or whether she feared how she would feel if he ever confirmed her suspicions.

She clung to the thought that once the baby was born they would be able to formalise some kind of arrangement. She would no longer need supervision as the woman carrying precious cargo and they would be able to work out visiting rights—a loose arrangement which would give her the freedom to get on with her life without him constantly intruding.

A sudden sharp twinge made her wince and she looked uncertainly at the mobile phone on the sofa next to her.

It was dark and cold outside, and a brisk wind was whipping a sharp drizzle against the windowpanes.

Inside, it was cosy and warm. Another twinge drove her from the sofa and she breathed deeply, tried to stay calm, because the baby wasn't due for another two and a half months and she didn't want to start panicking over every little twinge.

Neither did she want to ignore something that could be serious…

With a stifled gasp as another sharp pain in her stomach drove her from the sofa, she picked up the telephone and dialled through to Sergio. Just hearing his voice when he answered filled her with strength, and for a few seconds she almost regretted calling him.

'It's probably nothing...' she began.

About to manoeuvre across a roundabout, Sergio swung the car left, heading away from his apartment. He had picked up the fear in her voice with an ease that surprised him—although why it should, he had no idea. He seemed able to read nuances in her in a way he had never been able to with any other human being in his life before.

'What's probably nothing?'

'You're annoyed that I called, aren't you?'

'I'm annoyed that you're not telling me *why* you've called, but it doesn't matter because I'm already on my way and I'll be with you in twenty minutes.'

'No rush,' she managed through gritted teeth, knowing that he would rush. And in under fifteen minutes she heard the urgent ring of her doorbell.

'Tell me,' he commanded, staring down at her pale face and the brave smile she had pinned on it. Fear tore inside him. 'Okay, tell me on the way to the hospital.'

'There's no need...'

'I'll come back for that bag you packed. Come on.'

He was at his finest. Strong, calm...utterly in charge of the situation and knowing exactly what to do. She felt safe.

'Talk to me,' was the first thing he said once they were both in the car.

For the first time he wished that he had bought her somewhere with less of the illusion of being in the country and more of the reality of being in the hub of things— maybe even next to a hospital.

'I... Just a bit of pain,' she said faintly. 'My stomach.'

'Contractions? Like Braxton Hicks?'

'Sorry?'

'I thought it might be a good idea to do some background research,' Sergio told her gruffly.

She stared at his fierce averted profile in amazement.

'It's not that big a deal,' he asserted, without glancing in her direction. 'I like to know what I'm dealing with.'

'I don't know what it is, Sergio,' she whispered, 'but it just doesn't feel right.'

'Don't talk,' he urged in a low voice. 'Try and breathe evenly. The last thing you want to do is hyperventilate because you're panicked. I'm sure it's nothing to be unduly concerned about.'

'They hate you doing this.'

'What are you talking about?'

Susie leaned back against the headrest and closed her eyes. She was doing as he had told her to do, breathing evenly and thinking calming thoughts.

'The hospital. They hate it when you show up and they have to send you away again because it's a stupid false alarm. They're always rushed off their feet. It's a waste of their time when they have to pander to some pregnant woman who gets twitchy at the slightest...*ouch*...cramp...'

'No one would dare send me anywhere unless I was ready to go.'

He rested his hand on hers and gave a gentle squeeze, and she blinked back a flood of tears because right now she just loved him so much she wanted to shout it from the rooftops.

This felt so much like the real thing that she could almost believe it was.

'We're nearly there,' he said, removing his hand and leaving a cool, empty space where it had been.

Busy with trying to stave off the bursts of abdominal pain, Susie was actually only aware that they had arrived when the car stopped and she opened her eyes to find that he had pulled up right outside the hospital entrance. From then on, everything seemed to move very quickly.

He took charge. People obeyed. Nurses who were accustomed to giving orders fell into line with mesmerised obedience. A consultant was summoned.

'I should have made you go private,' he muttered at one point through gritted teeth. 'I should never have let you talk me into using the NHS…'

'Don't be silly. It's as good as…probably better…'

'You're as white as a sheet.'

'I…I'm a little scared, to be perfectly honest…' she admitted.

Voicing the fear suddenly made her realise that she was, in fact, terrified. What if she lost the baby?

Being established in a bed in the hospital, with people rushing around and someone urgently gathering the necessary team to do a scan in order to establish what was happening, really brought home to Susie just how much a part of her present and her future this unborn baby had become.

Sergio had temporarily disappeared, and a new and scary thought hit her with the force of a sledgehammer.

If she lost this precious possession, then he would disappear from her life faster than a speeding bullet.

There would be no need for him to stick around.

She would return the house she had fallen in love with, pack her bags and leave—because even though the house was in her name he would want it back. Why wouldn't he? It had been bought for his child, and for her as an afterthought.

She looked at him feverishly when he reappeared a few minutes later. She would have to make it clear that she understood the ramifications of what was happening and what might happen given a worst-case scenario.

'They're ready for you—and don't look so terrified.' He slanted a crooked smile at her. 'It'll be just fine.'

Susie nodded dumbly. *And if it's not?*

'It may not be,' she mumbled unsteadily. 'There are a thousand different things that could go wrong.'

'It isn't helpful to start looking for everything that could go wrong. Let's just hear what the consultant has to say. We'll know better how things stand once they scan you.'

Sergio was realising that he had lived a charmed life, casually assuming that whatever he wanted, he would get. The life of someone in complete control. He was realising that he had never felt *afraid*. He was feeling afraid now. She didn't have to tell him about all the things that could go wrong. He knew them all. He had done more than peruse that book he had bought. He had read it from cover to cover and could have written a thesis on mishaps that might occur.

'I can't help it,' Susie whispered. He had taken her hand in his and his fingers curled reassuringly around hers. 'I meant to ask you something...'

'What?'

Where the heck *were* these people? Shouldn't they be rushing around, taking care of this situation? Instead of slacking off at some workstation somewhere, gassing and telling jokes?

He forced down a sudden surge of anger and held on to what the consultant had told him: that in the absence of bleeding there was almost certainly no need to worry, that they would move as quickly as they could but that several unexpected emergencies had recently occurred, ensuring that all the available rooms for scanning were occupied.

'Have you found someone else?'

For a few seconds Sergio was dazed by the irrelevancy

of that question, but she was staring at him with wide-eyed earnestness, waiting for an answer.

'Where the heck did *that* come from?'

'It's just something that's been playing on my mind,' she said, breathing unevenly. 'And, while we're on the subject, I just want you to know that if you have there's no need to try and hide it from me.'

And no need for him to feel any responsibility or pity towards her if this pregnancy failed. Her thoughts were chaotic, but she had a sudden, pressing urge to make him understand that.

'This is not the time or the place to be having a nonsensical conversation like this,' Sergio told her roughly. 'Just concentrate on staying calm and optimistic.'

'I'm *very* calm and optimistic.'

'You're the most infuriatingly stubborn woman I've ever met. I don't suppose you're going to put this conversation to rest until I give you an answer, so I might as well oblige. Even though you *do* pick the most ridiculous moments to launch into your "Meaningful Conversations"...'

But maybe this was her way of distracting herself from negative thoughts about losing the baby—who was he to argue with her? He wasn't the one lying on a narrow, hard bed waiting for a scan...

He ran his fingers through her fine, silky, unruly hair and then cupped her face in a curiously tender gesture that made her feel as weak as a kitten.

'When the heck do you imagine I would have the time to find another woman?' he asked.

'Is that a no?'

'It's a no.'

'Because it's okay—you're a free man,' she pressed on feverishly.

'I get what you're saying.'

'I hope so, Sergio. Because if…if…'

Her voice wobbled, and there was no chance to say what she felt she *had* to say because they were interrupted by the arrival of a brisk nurse and the consultant. In the doorway, another nurse was waiting at the ready.

A room was now vacant but would not be for long, they were told on their way down in the lift.

'Never rains but it pours,' the consultant said wryly. 'Three heavily pregnant women with sudden complications and a couple of tricky caesareans—in addition to the usual range of deliveries. And Siamese twins tomorrow.' The consultant's face brightened at the prospect of that. 'You might have read about it recently? Right… Here we are… Nothing at all to worry about, Miss Sadler…'

He patted her hand kindly as she was transferred to a bed in the darkened room, but his attention was already on the scanning machine, caught up in the routine of what he needed to do.

Susie was keenly aware of Sergio next to her as she was prepped for the scan. She had not allowed him to go with her to any of her appointments. She wasn't sure why, but somewhere in the back of her mind she thought that it would have felt like another little surrender to the overwhelming love she felt for him. She had to keep some precious distance between them—had to preserve a little bit of neutrality or else get completely lost.

And she had always made sure to keep herself well covered. In fairness, she *had* increased in size, but not dramatically. But now, as her gown was opened so that the scan could begin, she was acutely conscious of the body she had so carefully hidden from him over the past few months.

She sneaked a glance at him and he caught her eyes in the darkened room and held them.

Now that she was lying on this bed it dawned on her that her pains had subsided considerably. *Typical.*

He leaned down so that he was speaking quietly into her ear. 'Stop thinking and just focus on the scan, Susie.'

Susie reddened and looked away. She stared at the monitor and tried hard to ignore her protruding, rounded belly.

Sergio, his gaze firmly fixed on the screen which had now been swivelled in their direction, marvelled that he could counsel *her* to stop thinking when he himself was caught up in a series of unwelcome thoughts.

What the heck did she mean by telling him that it was perfectly okay for him to entertain another woman? Was it her way of reminding him that she, likewise, was entitled to the freedom to entertain other men?

His eyes dropped briefly to her stomach, his first glimpse of her changed body, and possessiveness ripped through him.

She wouldn't look at another man now, but what about after the baby was born…?

She was swollen with *his child*—was she already contemplating the prospect of getting back into shape and meeting his replacement?

No. He refused to entertain that notion. Not here and not now.

He fixed all his attention on the picture presenting itself on the monitor and forgot all about the nagging anxieties playing at the back of his mind as the consultant took them through everything they were looking at—including the strong heartbeat which announced that everything was all right and there had been nothing to worry about after all.

'Always a good idea to get to hospital if you feel anything out of the ordinary,' he said kindly when, half an hour later, the lights were switched on and the gown, thankfully, was put back over her stomach.

'I panicked,' Susie confessed.

'Perfectly understandable,' the consultant told her. 'But everything seems to be in order. I should take it easy for the remainder of your pregnancy, though. Is there anyone staying with you—?'

'I'll be there,' Sergio interrupted, and Susie looked at him, open-mouthed.

He didn't look at her. He didn't have to in order to know exactly what she was thinking. That she wanted to preserve her independence and having him living with her under the same roof would be an appalling prospect.

Tough.

The consultant, already glancing at his watch, thinking ahead to his next appointment, was nodding and filling them in on the importance of making sure that she took it easy, didn't do anything that required too much exertion. Telling them that everything was fine, but that the human body had a cunning way of letting people know when things might be wrong.

And then, as fast as they had been swept up in the drama of the moment, they were on their own—free to leave the hospital.

'What did you mean when you told the consultant that you would be staying with me?' Susie asked abruptly.

For a while, when she had been focusing on the grainy little image of the baby, she had been wholly consumed, but now she was back to her anxious thoughts. She folded her arms and stared at him.

He might not have found someone else yet, but he would sooner or later—and how was she going to build up the strength to deal with that if he now intended to *move in*? She needed respite from his suffocating presence! The last thing she needed was to have him around all the time, reminding her that their relationship was not really a relationship.

But of course he would want to move in. Anything to protect his unborn child.

'Before we start on this conversation,' Sergio said, anticipating her mulish rejection of his offer, despite what the consultant had said, 'let's do the next patient a favour and vacate the room. We can talk about it on the way back to your house—and before you tell me that you're fine, and that there's no need for me to drop you home, forget it.'

'I wasn't going to say that.'

'Good. In that case, apologies for wrongly jumping the gun. And instead of thinking about my staying with you, and getting hot and bothered about the prospect, maybe we should both be happy that everything's okay?'

'Of course I'm happy.' Susie flushed, aware that he was right. 'Overjoyed. Even though I still feel like an idiot for rushing down here.'

'Like Mr Wilkins said, it's good to not take chances.'

'He was being polite.'

Heading towards the exit, Sergio controlled a frustrated smile. She always had an answer for everything. No one could ever accuse her of not being an everlasting source of challenge. If he pointed to the sky and told her that it looked blue, she would, given the right mood, argue that it was yellow, and she would continue arguing until she got bored and abandoned the conversation.

He had long ago congratulated himself on having reserves of patience that far surpassed anything he might have expected. Especially since now that she was pregnant she could be prone to being argumentative about nothing in particular.

'He's probably cursing at having to waste his precious time,' she rambled on, taking her time as she manoeuvred herself into his car. 'Pandering to a hypochondriac...'

As soon as they were both in the car, and he was slowly

threading his way through the car park out into the busy road, she turned to him.

'I realise, Sergio, that you're worried I might end up back in hospital because I've done something to overtire myself, but there's no cause for concern. I really am going to take things easy.'

'What do you mean, you *really are* going to take things easy? I thought you already were?'

'I've recently been doing some spring cleaning...'

'Spring cleaning *a new house*? What the heck is there to spring clean?'

'I brought some pictures down from Mum and Dad's house a couple of weeks ago,' she said vaguely. 'I've had a burst of energy lately so I've been putting them up here and there. In my studio and such. You know... Getting things homely.'

Sergio raked fingers through his hair and spared her a glance of pure frustration. 'Did that involve climbing on ladders?'

'Pregnant women climb on ladders all the time! In fact it's practically *all* they do.'

'And have you been eating when I haven't been there?'

Accustomed to living a life of complete independence— a life of frankly not giving a damn what other people thought of him—he was brought up short at the way it had been whittled away at the edges ever since she had announced that he was going to be a father. On the other hand, strength lay in the ability to adapt. He had adapted. It was a means to an end.

'Of course I have.'

But in between the sudden burst of spring cleaning energy and tying up the final bits of her commission she realised that food *had* taken a back seat. Or at least robust meals had—because when she was on the go crackers and cheese or sandwiches were always a faster option.

'I'll be moving in tomorrow. You've been overdoing things. And you may be prepared to take chances but I'm not. Let's get something clear right now. This isn't just *about you*. You're going to have to deal with that whether you like it or not.'

'But it's not necessary for you to move in!'

'I'll drop you back home and you can get some sleep. I'll be with you first thing in the morning to make sure that you eat your breakfast.'

'And do you intend to take time off work to supervise my lunches?'

'Now that you mention it, I can work from the house—so, in answer to your question, quite possibly. You want to behave like a child, then expect to be treated like one, Susie.'

'I haven't been behaving like a child and I don't want you around all the time, getting under my feet!'

Was that what he thought? That she was like a kid who needed to be told which road to follow because she was too simple to choose the right one? She hated the thought that she had gone from being the woman he wanted to someone he felt he had to *look after*. All his consideration for her over the past few months, she thought, had removed her sexuality.

'Too bad.' Sergio's voice hardened. 'Needs must.'

They drove the remainder of the way in silence. It was a quick drive, because at this hour the roads were clear. She knew that he would see her into the house, as indeed he did, and all the while she thought about him being there with her, living with her, sharing space with her, sitting in the little snug with her watching television.

She thought about the way they had been with one another before her pregnancy had forced him to put things into perspective. And then immediately her thoughts turned to when she had been lying on that narrow, uncomfortable bed in that room, being scanned, her stomach exposed to his gaze.

What had been going on in his mind then? Relief that they were no longer lovers? Impatience that he had had to come to the rescue because she was not independent enough to look after herself? Frustration that he had embarked on a light-hearted fling with someone out of his comfort zone just because he had liked her novelty value, only to find himself trapped with her for ever? Was he being forced to have her as an ongoing concern because of a child he hadn't wanted in the first place?

'So what time shall I expect you in the morning? Perhaps you could let me know how this arrangement is going to pan out?'

She contemplated him lurking in the house, materialising from dark corners, turning her on and distracting her, treating her like someone who couldn't look after herself. Treating her the way her parents and her sister treated her. When she thought like that she felt sick.

'Here's how it's going to pan out.' Sergio looked at her evenly. 'I'm going to set up camp in the downstairs den. There's a desk there already. It'll do for when I want to use it. I'll transfer over my desktop computer so that I have both my desktop and my laptop handy, and I'll arrange for a dedicated line to be put in so that you won't be plagued with calls coming through for me on your landline—although I can use my mobile well enough. How's it sounding so far?'

'Constricting,' Susie said with utter dejection.

He frowned at her. 'You have the night to get used to the prospect.'

'I've become accustomed to peace and quiet.'

'I'll make sure not to play my trumpet too loudly. You'll thank me when this baby is delivered fat and healthy.'

And then? she thought. What happens then? She would have become accustomed to having him around. She knew that because she was already accustomed to having him around now and he wasn't even living with her.

'And shall I...er...? Well, I feel I ought to ask this... what about sleeping arrangements?' she asked in a rush.

They found themselves in the kitchen and she sank into a chair and looked at him.

'What about them?'

Just like that his mind swung back to the sight of her on that bed, the bigness of her stomach, her belly button slightly protruding—the essence of the rounded, fertile woman. *His woman.*

Except she wasn't, was she?

Currently she was a woman who was trying to have a conversation about the boundaries she could put into place to spare herself the discomfort of having him under her feet. His mouth tightened, but he wasn't going to get involved in a row with her. Stress came in different guises, and he wasn't going to stress her by arguing with her— especially not now.

Marriage was no longer a subject under discussion. It had been efficiently and silently removed from the menu. Should he have pressed home his point in the beginning? Left her with no wriggle room? Because if they had got married he would have been able to keep an eye on her... they wouldn't have ended up racing to the hospital in a state of flat-out panic.

But a reluctant, bitter and resentful wife...? No, the answer did not lie there.

Nevertheless, reluctant and resentful as she might be

at his intrusion into her happy, solitary and peaceful existence here, it was still going to happen.

'There are four bedrooms in this house, Susie...' He couldn't veil the simmering frustration that had crept into his voice at the thought of, for the first time in his life, planting himself somewhere where he wasn't wanted. 'I don't think it will be an insurmountable problem if I use one of them. And if memory serves me right there are two en suite bathrooms, so there will be no danger of our crossing paths first thing in the morning with toothbrushes in our hands.'

Susie blushed, guiltily aware that he was putting himself out for her and doing it without complaint. It would be a far more laborious commute for him to get to work in the mornings, and if he chose to work from the house, that too would be a huge sacrifice.

Why did she always emerge feeling like the villain in the piece?

Because she wanted so much more from him, and wanting more made her edgy...made her sound ungrateful for the little things he did...even for the big things he did. Because, however big they were, they weren't big enough.

'Just relax about it, Susie. It's no big deal and it won't be for long.'

'Because when the baby's born you'll clear out?'

'What else would you want?' he asked brusquely.

For a heartbeat, she played with the idea of throwing caution to the winds and telling him that actually what she wanted was a ring on her finger and him in bed beside her every night, for them to grow old together. What she wanted was for him to be madly in love with her, and it would be weak and stupid ever to think of settling for anything less.

But when she thought of him tonight...the way his safe,

solid presence had taken away all her fears and made her feel secure…

'Good. Okay.'

'I'll even take the load from your shoulders by helping with the cooking,' he said, and shot her a slanting smile that set her whole body alight.

'Is that a threat or a promise?'

'You have my solemn word that I'll consult recipe books before I decide to fling a few things into a pan.'

'I guess it would be nice to have somebody cook for me.'

She was a woman built to share her life with someone, and that fact was brought forcibly home to him when she said that, her voice wistful. Hard on the heels of that thought came a less pleasant one, and that was that the person she would end up sharing her life with wouldn't be him—even though between them they had created the new life growing in her stomach.

'No stress. Remember what the consultant said? And I don't like the thought of you spending hours in that studio of yours, doing painstaking work.'

'I move around a lot,' Susie confessed. 'I draw and paint a little, and then I stretch my legs and wander around the house to make sure my muscles don't decide to seize up on me. Besides, I'm nearly finished with my commission, and the next one is for a children's book so it'll be far less detailed. In fact I shall probably be able to do a lot of it in front of the telly. Sergio, there's no need for you to feel that you have to micromanage every single aspect of my life because I'm pregnant.'

Sergio ignored that. 'Are you all right to stay on your own tonight?'

'Of course I am—and that's just what I'm talking about!' She took a deep breath. 'In fact,' she said evenly,

'I'm so tired I shall probably fall asleep the second my head hits the pillow.'

Unlike all those other times, when bed had signalled a lot more than falling asleep.

A rush of jumbled thoughts crowded into her head, jostling for space. Memories of being touched by him combined with the stress of the past few hours, the security she had felt at having him at her side, the relief at having received the all-clear…the sadness of realising that he truly saw her as nothing more than a responsibility, the helplessness at wanting more and knowing she would never have it.

Her eyes darkened and she licked suddenly dry lips. He was staring at her and she was rooted to the chair, unable to move a muscle. Except for her heart. Her heart was the only thing moving, beating inside her so fast and so hard that she wanted to faint.

'Don't,' Sergio warned her gruffly.

She blinked at him in an attempt to clear her head. 'Don't what?'

'Don't look at me like that.' He shook his head, broke eye contact briefly, but then was compelled to look at her again.

'Like what?'

'Like you're issuing an invitation.'

Or maybe he had misread that expression on her face? Before he had always had complete and utter confidence in his ability to have whatever woman he wanted, but she had managed to instil in him a healthy vein of self-doubt.

'You're tired,' he continued. 'We're both exhausted after tonight.'

'Which means…' she was angry with herself again, because she had only just managed to catch herself before she fell headlong into what would have been a stupid mistake '…that it's time for you to leave.'

She hazarded a smile, which seemed to do the trick, breaking the spell between them and allowing her to breathe as though something heavy *wasn't* sitting on her chest. She stood up and began walking him to the front door, keeping her distance.

It was bad enough that she would have to fight her feelings for him without the luxury of having time out when he wasn't around, but how much worse if she had given in? If she had done what her body had been urging her to do? If she had just…stepped towards him, laid her palm on his hard chest, stripped off her jumper and her thick thermal vest and her sensible bra so that he could swirl his tongue over her sensitive nipples…?

How uncomfortable would *that* have made the situation? Because he would have responded. She had glimpsed the flare of hunger in his eyes. And maybe he was just horny because he hadn't had sex in a while, or maybe he was curious to find out what it felt like to make love to a woman who was big with his child, but he *would* have responded…

And then in the morning he would no longer have been horny, and would no longer have been curious, and where would *that* have left them?

She heard herself talking normally to him as she showed him out, even though her mind was in a whirl, and when he had gone she leaned against the front door and finally allowed herself to breathe evenly.

How the heck was she going to survive the next couple of months? she wondered.

CHAPTER TEN

'I THINK I felt something...'

Sergio looked up from the report he had been scanning on his computer. Sometimes he found it hard to believe that he was the same man who had wined and dined women, slept with them, moved on... The same man whose entire life had been focused on work and the thrill of making money and growing an empire. A man who had enjoyed the freedom of living exclusively for himself.

He had moved in with her seven weeks previously and they had settled into a routine which was one born of necessity. He knew that. Of course he did. Circumstances had compelled him to live life at a pace he would never have imagined possible. What made him uneasy was the fact that he had adapted so fast.

They were living in a weird kind of bubble, in which they functioned as a couple for the sake of their unborn child. Bubbles eventually burst. When this one did the dithering would be over and she would accept the inevitable. He had indulged her by not forcing her hand, but in the end the result would be the same.

Except now the certainty that this was going to work out as planned seemed to hang in the balance, and he felt a rare surge of confusion.

'No, it's nothing.'

Susie had been frankly terrified of this arrangement, and sometimes when she thought about it she was still terrified—because she had become so accustomed to sharing space with him. Had he been right all along? That a marriage of convenience would be a workable marriage? Had she made far too big a deal of wanting the fairy tale of love and romance and assuming that anything that fell short of that was a waste of time?

'You're becoming the queen of the false alarm,' Sergio said drily, flipping shut his laptop and standing to stretch out his muscles, which had tightened from sitting in one place for too long.

He had gone into the office today, had successfully signed on the dotted line for a deal that had been brewing for nearly a year and a half, and yet his only thoughts had been of how fast he could get back to her.

He looked at her broodingly and she met his gaze and then glanced away.

This happened a lot less than she had feared…this flipping over of her heart when their eyes met and held for a fraction too long…when she happened to see something in his gaze that spoke of other stuff…not just the normal, casual, comfortable stuff that passed between them from day to day.

It was like looking down into a clear stream and glimpsing the swirl of dangerous currents moving so fast and so deep that they didn't ruffle the calm surface except very occasionally, when they glittered and seduced and held her temporarily captive.

Dry-mouthed, she dragged her eyes away from him, half wishing that he wouldn't stand there, stretching, so that his shirt tugged free from the waistband of his trousers, exposing a sliver of bronzed flat belly that tempted her fingers.

'I know…' Her breath hitched in her throat. 'Every time I feel anything I think I'm about to go into labour—even though the midwife's told me a hundred times that it's only labour if I can time the contractions. Getting something that feels like a contraction every other day doesn't count.'

'You'd be forgiven for getting panicky—especially in light of that scare…not to mention the fact that the baby's due any day now.'

'I know. It's come round so quickly since…since…'

'Since you sprang it on me?'

His voice was low and serious, and for some reason she felt a little thread of alarm race through her because this was as serious as he had been since… Well, since he had moved in.

The intimacy of their shared situation settled like a weight on her. It was pitch-black outside. Dinner had been eaten, dishes stacked in the dishwasher, and she was a handful of minutes away from heading upstairs for the night, leaving Sergio in the sitting room. He would resume work and then would retire to bed at some point during the night or the early hours of the morning.

Winter was all around them. The homely warmth of the house kept it at bay, but as he continued to look at her she was aware of the fact that, yes, there really were only the two of them in this place. Ex-lovers who had created a baby between them… Herself and the man she was compelled to look at, driven to want…

She licked her lips and set aside the little sketch pad on which she had been drawing.

'I…er…' She cleared her throat and looked at him. 'I've never thanked you for being so decent about the whole thing. Your whole life's been turned on its head.' She laughed. 'Can you believe that this is the first time we're really talking about this?'

'There seemed little point in stressing you out with long-winded discussions...' Eyes still pinned to her face, Sergio strolled to one of the chairs facing the sofa and sat down, hunching forward so that his forearms were resting on his thighs.

But now the time had come to talk. He wasn't sure how long this had been building inside him, how long he had known that the comfortable arrangement they had fallen into would have to be broken. He just knew that the baby would be born any day now and that once that baby arrived the situation between them would change dramatically.

Opportunities would be lost for ever.

Suddenly opportunities and having access to them seemed like the most important thing in the world. So this was it. Naturally they had to talk. They couldn't walk blindly into parenthood without first sorting out all the little details that would crash into them the second this baby was born. They had to be prepared. *She* had to be prepared. And this so-called conversation was going to stress her out.

'I know you think I've needed watching over ever since the scare at the hospital, but I don't,' Susie said flatly.

Restlessness washed into her. She wondered whether she should mention that her stress levels were building—and then decided that her stress levels would rocket whenever they had this conversation, be it here and now, or next week, or when she was lying in a hospital bed with their baby in a crib next to them.

There was never going to be a right time to hear what had to be said, because she had become so accustomed to having him around.

'You can't blame a guy for being concerned. You are, after all, carrying my child.'

'Shall I tell you something? I never thought you were

the sort of conventional person who'd ever come out with
stuff like that.'

'I'm glad to have introduced you to a new side of my
personality.'

'I've seen lots of different sides of your personality over
the past few weeks…'

'Should I be uneasy when you say that?'

'You said that we needed to talk.'

'I don't remember putting it quite like that.'

'Not in so many words…' She shrugged. 'But I've de-
veloped a knack for reading between the lines.' She sighed
and sifted her fingers through her hair. 'I guess this is as
good a time as any to decide what…what's going to happen once the baby's born. It needs to be out in the open. I
mean, there are all sorts of decisions to be made.'

'Yes. There are.'

'For starters, you've got a life to lead—a life that's waiting out there for you.'

'What makes you think that you know what sort of life
is out there waiting for me to lead it?'

'I feel like you've been forced to put your whole life on
hold to move in here with me. It's been a sacrifice.'

'For you?' Sergio drawled. 'Or for me?'

'For…both of us…'

But since when was it a great sacrifice to be living with
the guy you loved, who was looking out for you? Taking care of you? What pregnant woman *didn't* want to be
treated like a piece of china? If she could only box up all
the other anxieties that went along with that scenario…

Sergio flushed darkly. He wondered when his priorities
had shifted and marvelled that he had failed to pay due attention to this sea change. He had mistakenly thought that
the bombshell had been her pregnancy. He'd been wrong.
The fog of confusion he had earlier dismissed returned

and then cleared, and in the clear light he could see the precipice over which he was dangling.

She was fidgeting, her fingers playing with the cotton of her loose jogging bottoms. She had only just conceded in the past couple of weeks that she needed proper maternity wear. Before that she had banked on elasticated waistbands to do the trick.

'It's been worth it, hasn't it? Having me here?'

'You can be very reassuring.'

'Is that all you have to say on the subject?'

'What *else* is there to say?' Susie cried, suddenly wanting this dreadful conversation to be over and done with, and angry with him for drawing it out with pointless questions.

The businesslike arrangement he so approved of might have taken a bit of a knock, but she wanted him to bring it back to the table now, so that she could get her head around it before the baby came.

'Do you want me to present you with a medal because you took time out of your hectic lifestyle to supervise me and make sure I wasn't getting up to anything that might harm the baby?'

'I'm not looking for medals.' Maybe this wasn't the time to be having this conversation after all. 'And I don't want to stress you out, Susie. That's not my intention.'

'I'm not stressed out.'

She breathed evenly, deeply, clearing her head and trying to fight her way past the fog of unhappiness that threatened to smother her—because she didn't want to think about what was going to happen tomorrow, or next week, or at the end of the month. She wanted to wallow in the present and, yes, pretend that the present wasn't going to turn into the future. She wanted to be a coward for a little bit longer.

'And there's no need for you to be so darn gentle with me, Sergio. I'm not going to fall apart at the seams just because you want to clear the air and sort out the details before life gets busy with a baby. I want that too! So—you'll move out and you can come and visit as often as you like. You'd just have to give me notice. I don't want you showing up out of the blue and expecting a cup of coffee. I know you bought the house, and I know right now you have a key, but I'll expect you to return the key when you leave. For good.'

She was holding herself ramrod-stiff. The deep breathing obviously had a way to go when it came to relaxing her. It didn't augur well for labour.

'Right.'

'And I'm sure we can work out something sensible with the financial side of things. I mean, the arrangement we have at the moment seems to be working all right—and, of course, the more established I get in my freelance work, the less dependent I'll be on you...'

'Right.'

Her words were floating around his head without really registering. He was staring down into an abyss and for the first time in his life was paralysed with inaction. How was it that he hadn't spotted the ground opening up beneath his feet? He had never in his entire life taken his eye off the ball, but he had done it with her.

'And then you can get back to your busy life. I don't know... Would you want me to sign anything?'

'My busy life...?'

'Earning money, running an empire, being a mover and a shaker in the big, bad world...'

Over time she had come to grasp not just the extent of his wealth but the extent of his power and influence. Neither impressed her, because if he'd been poorer and less influential, then maybe he would have wanted what she wanted: just a normal relationship. Maybe he would have loved her the way she loved him. She didn't enjoy thinking like that, but she couldn't help it.

'I seem to have taken quite a bit of time out of my "busy life" over the past few weeks, wouldn't you agree?'

'But I didn't force you to—'

'Did I say that you did?'

'No, but—'

'Did it ever occur to you that I may have *wanted* to?'

'For the baby,' Susie inserted hastily, before her heart had time to pick up speed and before her head could start building castles in the sky.

'Love… It comes with a lot of high hopes and bitter disappointments…'

'I know that's how *you* feel.'

'Or so I thought.' He ran his fingers through his hair—a gesture that was part frustration, part weird nerves. 'My father had a long and successful marriage with my mother and it was a marriage that was arranged. When he flung himself headlong into love it crashed and burned.'

'His marriage might have been arranged, but has it ever occurred to you that he fell in love with your mother? That what he felt for his second wife wasn't love at all? Maybe just a reaction to loneliness? He was weak and he fell for a pretty woman who flattered him. It happens. But it isn't love.'

'I *have* been doing some thinking, and for the first time…'

For the first time he had thought of his parents, remembered the way they had been with one another, and had realised, slowly but surely, that what had begun as an arrangement had ended as true love. The story hadn't been as black and white as he had imagined. He had always equated marriage as an arrangement as successful and marriage as a whirlwind of emotion and so-called love as a nightmare. It had subtly altered his approach to relationships.

'For the first time...?'

'This situation between us isn't going to work, Susie,' he said roughly.

It felt as though he was on the edge of a cliff, a yawning drop at his feet, but the thing was that he was going to step off the side—whatever the outcome.

'You don't want to be married to me—you see that as some sort of unacceptable sacrifice, where the only inevitable outcome would be both of us being miserable and resentful...'

'You would miss your freedom.' She stared down at her fingers while her mind darted like quicksilver in a thousand different directions.

'I would miss you more.' Their eyes met and he found that he was holding his breath. 'We *work*. I challenge you to deny that. We can live together and it's good between us. And that's without sex.'

'What are you saying?'

'I don't want you on a part-time basis when the baby's born. Just think about it. Think about what we have. This isn't a relationship that's destined to fail just because it's been generated by the fact that you became pregnant. Maybe that was Fate. I've never been much of a believer in that old chestnut, but lately I've had a turnaround. Fate brought us together and it conspired to keep us together—and that's what I want. To be with you. With you both. You and our baby.'

'I don't understand...' Because missing from all of that were the three words she wanted to hear.

'I'm not the sort of guy you ever saw as a long-term

proposition…but Susie, I *could* be. I mean, think about it—have we had one argument since I moved in? A single argument? No. Not one. Have I been…well…*useful*? Yes. Those are two things you should take into account when you decide that I'm not the one for you. You might fantasise about someone who wears an earring, has a ponytail and knows how to cook quiche, but would he really be the man for you?'

'He might be if he loved me…'

'No one could love you as much as I do. *No one.*'

'You *love* me? No, you don't. You don't believe in love.'

Unable to tell her what he was being driven to tell her without touching her, Sergio took immediate advantage of her open-mouthed confusion to join her on the sofa. If he had to overwhelm her with his physical proximity, then so be it. He wasn't above low tricks.

'I never thought I did,' he murmured, 'but no one's right all of the time. Even me.'

'Now I really *am* shocked.' Susie's heart was swooping and diving so fast that she could scarcely breathe. 'I thought you were the guy who never got it wrong?'

'You're going to marry me,' he ordered shakily. 'Aren't you?'

Susie pulled him towards her and kissed him with all the passion she had been storing up for the past weeks and months—the passion that had lain slumbering under the surface, ever ready to leap out and take charge.

'You love me! Of *course* I'm going to marry you. I've loved you for so long… I just never thought that you could ever love me back—and I've been so scared of getting used to you being around me. You never thought that you could love, and I always knew that I could…except I never expected it to be someone like you…'

'I'm reading all sorts of terrific compliments into that,' Sergio said huskily.

He slipped his hand under the jumper and gently, tenderly caressed her, stroked her swollen nipples, but he didn't go further. They had a lifetime to explore one another. He could take his time. But he just had to feel her, and her body was wonderfully familiar. Everything about her filled him with a sense of completion, as though this was the woman he had been waiting to find.

He shuddered when he thought that he might not have met her at all—that she might have joined that mustard-clothed clown on her blind date and left his restaurant without throwing herself into his company.

'You should,' Susie whispered. 'And you should know something else…'

'What's that?'

'I feel a twinge—and this time it's the real thing…'

Georgina Louise Francesca Burzi was born with very little fuss, after a complication-free delivery. Pink-cheeked, with a mop of dark curls, dark eyes and the same long dark killer eyelashes of her father, she was declared by every single person who came to visit the most beautiful baby on the planet.

Louise Sadler, chuffed to bits with the impending wedding—which, she declared, she had always known would happen, because what mother *didn't* know when her daughter was in love—made time to gloat quietly over the fact that she had hit the grandmother post first.

'And leave the wedding to me,' she added sotto voce, keeping a sharp eye on her husband, who was holding the baby and attempting to look comfortable. 'I'm suggesting small, intimate and exquisite—emphasis on the *exquisite*. Too big can sometimes be just a little too tacky…'

Susie was more than happy to oblige, and she realised, somewhere deep inside her, how far she had come. She was no longer trying to prove anything to any of her family. They loved her as she was...

And so did Sergio—who never tired of telling her.

Now, with their visitors all gone and back in the comfort of their house, Susie reached out and linked her fingers through his, settling with a sigh into the gentle kiss he placed on her neck. In a Moses basket next to the sofa, where they were sitting quietly relaxing, baby Georgie was sleeping, her tiny, soft snores punctuating the comfortable silence.

In three months' time they would be having their delayed honeymoon—baby and all.

For now...

She rested her head in the crook of his neck and then raised her upturned face to his and smiled, before kissing him gently on the mouth—a sweet, long kiss that expressed more than words could ever begin to say.

I love you...I want you...I need you...and I always will.

* * * * *

COMING NEXT MONTH FROM

HARLEQUIN *Presents*®

Available July 21, 2015

#3353 CHATSFIELD'S ULTIMATE ACQUISITION
The Chatsfield
by Melanie Milburne
Isabelle Harrington is *furious* when arrogant playboy Spencer Chatsfield becomes her new boss. He's also the man who shattered her heart years ago. The only thing she can't stand more than Spencer is the sizzling chemistry *still* burning between them!

#3354 THE GREEK DEMANDS HIS HEIR
The Notorious Greeks
by Lynne Graham
Leo Zikos is pleased to have secured a perfectly *convenient* fiancée, until Grace Donovan's impeccable beauty tempts him to pursue one last night of freedom... But that night, and the positive pregnancy test that follows, blows Leo's plans apart!

#3355 HIS SICILIAN CINDERELLA
Playboys of Sicily
by Carol Marinelli
Matteo Santini bought one night with Bella Gatti to protect her innocence, but then she disappeared. Now, forced together at a wedding, he wants a reckoning. The only way Bella will be leaving the party is with Matteo—via his bed!

#3356 THE PERFECT CAZORLA WIFE
by Michelle Smart
Charley Cazorla strides back into her soon-to-be ex-husband's life with a plan. Except Raul has his own ideas! To save Charley's business, the Spaniard demands his own payment: she must resume her role as the *perfect* wife—in *every* sense!

HPCNM0715RA

#3357 THE SINNER'S MARRIAGE REDEMPTION
Seven Sexy Sins
by Annie West

Flynn Marshall is determined to rush stunning Ava Cavendish to the altar at the first opportunity. A trophy bride should complete his plans, but the desire Ava inflames in this untouchable CEO soon turns his ordered strategy on its head...

#3358 THE MARAKAIOS BABY
The Marakaios Brides
by Kate Hewitt

Margo Ferras knows that she must give up devishly seductive Leo Marakaios in order to protect her heart. But when she discovers that she's pregnant with his child, Margo walks back into Leo's life and asks *him* to marry *her*!

#3359 CAPTIVATED BY THE GREEK
by Julia James

Salesgirl Mel may not be Nikos Parakis's type, but she can't resist his tempting offer: a no-strings romance under the sizzling sun. But parting ways is made impossible when sultry nights with the captivating Greek leave Mel carrying his heir!

#3360 CLAIMED FOR HIS DUTY
Greek Tycoons Tamed
by Tara Pammi

Stavros Sporades agreed to marry heiress Leah Huntington to protect her, but now she's demanding a divorce! Stavros wants proof Leah's troubled past is behind her, but one night of desire reveals that she might have been innocent all along...

YOU CAN FIND MORE INFORMATION ON UPCOMING HARLEQUIN® TITLES, FREE EXCERPTS AND MORE AT WWW.HARLEQUIN.COM.

HPCNM0715RB

REQUEST YOUR
FREE BOOKS!

HARLEQUIN

Presents

2 FREE NOVELS PLUS
2 FREE GIFTS!

SPECIAL EXCERPT FROM

HARLEQUIN

Presents

*Does Charley Cazorla dare return to her husband's
bed? Does she even have a choice, when Raul is
offering a deal she really can't refuse…?*

*Read on for an exclusive excerpt of this stunning
new book by* **Michelle Smart**
THE PERFECT CAZORLA WIFE

"It won't happen again," she promised through ragged
breaths.

"I think you've told enough lies this past week, don't
you?"

Raul sat back down, waiting for the thunder beneath
his rib cage to abate.

How had things gotten out of hand so quickly?

He'd been taunting her, teasing her, asserting his
control, spelling out to her how much he held the upper
hand. He'd enjoyed it but had kept his mind firmly on the
seduction in hand.

She'd been the one to kiss him, a fact that, from the
look on her face, she regretted hugely.

She'd hooked her arm around his neck and his mind
had gone blank, desire overshadowing everything else.

The chemistry between them had always been explosive, but that…

It had felt as if a coil locked in a too-tight box had
finally sprung free.

He'd been seconds away from taking her on the table.

She still stood there, her green eyes firing their hatred at him.

Whom did she hate the most? Him for compelling her back into his bed? Or herself for wanting it?

"So, *cariño*, do we have a deal?" He was gratified to hear his voice functioning as normal. He would *never* allow himself to show weakness in front of her. "The day care centre, signed, sealed, delivered and renovated in exchange for four months in my bed?"

Four months. That would surely be enough to get her out of his system once and for all.

Maybe it was fortuitous that she'd walked back into his life at this moment. He needed to move on, not just from the dissolution of their marriage but from the sexual hold she still held over him.

Her chin rose, her pretty nostrils flaring. "Yes. I accept your terms, but with one condition of my own—I won't be sharing your bed until the deeds of the building are in my hands."

"The building will be in the Cazorla name by the end of the week."

"Then you'll have to wait until then before you can touch me again."

"You are not in a position to make any demands, *cariño*."

Don't miss
THE PERFECT CAZORLA WIFE by Michelle Smart,
available August 2015 wherever
Harlequin Presents® books and ebooks are sold.

www.Harlequin.com

HPEXP0715